Peacekeepers

Peacekeepers

Dianne Linden

COTEAU BOOKS
WWW.COTEAUBOOKS.COM

Edited by Barbara Sapergia.
Cover and text illustrations by Susan Gardos.
Cover and book design by Duncan Campbell.
Printed and bound in Canada at AGMV Marquis.

National Library of Canada Cataloguing in Publication Data

Linden, Dianne
Peacekeepers / Dianne Linden.

ISBN 1-55050-271-9

1. Bullying—Juvenile fiction. I. Title.
PS8573.I51P42 2003   jC813'.6   C2003-911240-3

10 9 8 7 6 5 4 3 2

COTEAU BOOKS
401-2206 Dewdney Ave
Regina, Saskatchewan
Canada   s4R 1H3

available in Canada and the US from:
Fitzhenry & Whiteside
195 Allstate Parkway
Markham, Ontario
Canada   L3R 4T8

The publisher gratefully acknowledges the financial assistance of the Saskatchewan Arts Board, the Canada Council for the Arts, the Government of Canada through the Book Publishing Industry Development Program (BPIDP), and the City of Regina Arts Commission, for its publishing program.

For all kids who go to school lonely or frightened.
You are braver than you know.

Subject: **Sherlock and Watson**
Date: October 27, 2000 22:15:22
From: "MCpl.AS.Mackelwain,ASU Edmonton,
582 5418,0900" <mail466@dnd.ca>
To: mmackelwain@hotmail.com

Dear Nell and Lester B.,

I just got back from Zagreb with a truck full of medical supplies. It's late, but I want you to have this tomorrow, so you'll know that I'm doing well. I also want to tell you about two new members of the de-mining team here. They're German Shepherds, and their names are Sherlock and Watson. They've been donated by the Canadian government to help clear areas like schoolyards and farmers' fields of land mines.

It's really fascinating to watch them work. First the human members of the team stake out the space they're clearing, in rows a metre wide, and mark each one with red flags. Explosive material seeps out of buried land mines and the dogs can smell it, so they slowly sniff their way down the rows. When they detect a scent, they go into a quiet sit, and the human mine clearers move in. Sherlock and Watson don't disturb the ground and have never been hurt themselves.

There are around one hundred mine-detecting dogs here now, and most of their handlers are local people. That means that every day a little bit more Bosnian countryside is safe for people to walk on again.

I hope I'll be able to call you soon at a time when you're home and still awake.

Love you and miss you,

Mom
"MCpl.AS.Mackelwain,ASU Edmonton,582-5418,0900"
e-mail:466@dnd.ca

Chapter One

*I*t's Monday, the last period of the morning, and I'm in my Foods class. There are three other people at the food-prep station where I work. Sam Hashi and Priscilla Wong are both in Grade Seven like me. Priscilla is serious about school. She pays a lot of attention to doing her assignments well, and writes down practically everything that happens in class in very tiny, very neat handwriting.

Sam is tall for his age, with dark eyes and dark curly hair. All he ever says to me is stuff like, "Could I please have the egg beater?" or "Have you seen the measuring spoons?" Once he remarked about the French toast being pretty good. But I appreciate the fact that he's polite. That's something I can't say about the fourth person in our group.

Shane Morrison is in Grade Eight. He isn't as tall as Sam, and he's got kind of a baby face, but he's managed to produce a shadow of a moustache on his upper lip. Add that to the sneer he usually has on his face and the slouchy way he walks, and it's obvious he's fast-tracking his way through puberty so he can become a threat to society as soon as possible. After you've heard everything I have to say about him, you may think that time has already arrived.

If you say hi to Shane, which I don't but lots of people do, or if he even sees you looking at him, he holds up his hands like he has talons on them and rips them through the air while he gnashes his teeth. It's all very macho, and makes you wonder why he would want to be in a class that teaches kids how to cook. Also, why he was allowed to register.

I heard him tell someone that there wasn't enough space for him to take Foods last year and he felt ripped off, so his parents made a big stink about it. I wouldn't have thought a person like Shane had parents, except, maybe, a couple of rocks, but apparently he does. And I guess it's possible they actually care about nutrition and all that, but it's for sure Shane doesn't. All he does is stand around and boss the rest of us, eat most of what we cook, and then complain about how it tastes afterwards.

Shane never pays any attention to Priscilla. And Sam seems to know him from somewhere, so while they're not exactly friends, they get along. I'm the lucky person Shane's chosen to pick on in our group. He's been doing it since the first day of class.

At first he just called me "Midget," because I'm on the short side. That didn't bother me a lot, because my legs are long and strong for my height, and also I figure I still have time to grow. My mom says that's how things went for her. Next he started calling me "Nellie," which really is my name. I absolutely hate it, though, and I've told him so at least a dozen times. After that it was "Smelly," which was embarrassing and also not true. I shower and wear clean clothes every day. Now, every time he sits down, he does this sniffing thing in my direction.

He's gone through my purse several times – once he even took out my family pictures and waved them around. "They're all geeks!" he said, before I grabbed them back.

Then last week he got even more personal. We were watching a video on kitchen safety and taking notes. I could tell Shane was staring at me and I tried to ignore him, but finally I put down my pencil and looked up. He did his claw thing and stared at me like he'd just come back from an island where he'd been hunting with panthers and tigers, and hadn't been with humans for many years. He opened out his thumb and index finger as if they were tweezers and pretended to pick something up off the table. Then he made a big show of examining it closely.

"Is that mouse hair?" he asked in a raspy whisper. He held his fingers up next to my head. "Oh, sorry," he said. "I guess it's yours."

That really got me. Everyone in my family has curly red hair. Mom's and my little brother Mikey's are kind of auburn. My Uncle Martin's is more of a carroty colour. I should say, everyone in my family has red hair, except me. Mine is light brown and kind of fine and wispy – mousy, I guess you could say – which is obviously the point Shane's trying to make. I keep my hair short, which is trendy, and my mom tells me it has interesting texture. But when I take off my toque in winter and my hair's standing on end with static – while hers and Mikey's is shiny and well-behaved, and even Uncle Martin's long, red ponytail is under control – I could just scream.

In fact, sometimes I do. I may not be a redhead, but I do have a redhead's temper, and for the past few months I've really been having a hard time hanging on to it. When Shane made that dig about my hair, it took all the self-control I could come up with to clamp my jaws together and look back at the video.

He wouldn't let it go, though. He moved his fingers over in front of Sam's face. "Doesn't this look like mouse hair to you, Sam?" he asked. Sam looked down at his paper and didn't say anything.

By then I couldn't keep quiet any longer. "How do you know it's not yours?" I hissed back, pointing to his upper lip. "You used to have more than six hairs in your moustache, didn't you?" I tried to sneer, but I don't know if I managed it. "Have you ever thought about taking vitamins? They make chewy ones especially for children."

Shane narrowed his eyes and leaned in to say something else, when Mr. Melnyk glided over and told us to get to work. He's our Foods teacher. "There are many important points in this video," he said. Then he tapped Shane's paper, which had nothing on it except the drawing of a hand with claws dripping blood.

"What's this got to do with kitchen safety?" he asked. He took Shane's note sheet away, got a new one, plunked it down in front of him and said, "I'll need to see this at the end of class."

After Mr. Melnyk moved on, Shane gave me the rogue animal look again. "You'd better be careful, Smelly," he said, "I can make your life miserable."

"I don't think so," I said back, which goes to show what I know about anything.

*L*ike I say, that was last week. Today is the day before Halloween. Mr. Melnyk likes to do things with us that are seasonally appropriate, so we're making pumpkin muffins. Some kids make fun of him and complain that the thematic stuff we do in Foods is babyish, but personally, I don't hold Mr. Melnyk's enthusiasm against him. He's my teacher for Language Arts as well as Foods and he manages to look like he's awake in both classes, which is more than I can say for most of the teachers at JAWS. That's what I call James A. Wyndotte School, where I've been a very unhappy student since September.

Anyway, we're making muffins, like I said. I'm getting the dry ingredients ready and Sam and Priscilla are breaking the eggs and doing all the other wet stuff. Shane is watching and heckling, as usual. I bend over to get the sifter from the bottom shelf of the cupboard, and he comes up really close behind me, leans over, and says in my ear, "I'm looking down your shirt, and there's nothing there." I stand up really fast and apparently hit his chin with the back of my head.

I want to say something smart, but smart words don't come. In the first place, Shane is dabbing at a cut on his bottom lip and throwing a lot of four letter words in my direction. In the second place, the fact that he's been so close to me makes me feel like throwing up. So even though I know that ratting on other students just leads to more trouble – even though I know it would be smarter to just apologize and back off – I make a beeline for Mr. Melnyk. He's on the other side of the room showing two kids how to arrange pumpkin seeds on their muffin tops.

"I can't work with him any more!" I say, pointing at Shane. "He's an animal!"

Mr. Melnyk opens up his hands and lets the pumpkin seeds plop down off his fingers onto the last muffin top. He sighs, straightens up, and looks over at Shane.

"She butted me in the mouth with her head," he whines. "You're not supposed to allow violence in this school." I'm sure his lip is a little swollen by now, but I also think he's sticking it out to make it look worse than it is.

Mr. Melnyk gives me his "I'm-Waiting-to-Hear-Your-Side" look, and I ask to speak to him privately. We walk over into the area of the room where the washer and dryer are. I haven't been sharing much with anybody lately, but now that my mouth is working again, I just get out of the way and let it take over.

"For the last couple of weeks," I say, "Shane's been bug-ging me continually. He calls me names and says insulting things I wouldn't care to repeat. He never does any work.

And he constantly criticizes us and eats everything we cook."

Now that I've started, it feels okay talking to Mr. Melnyk. I can hear the towels and washcloths whirling around in the dryer while we talk, and it's kind of homey in the laundry corner. I do find the smell of certain fabric softeners very comforting.

I tell him how Shane took pictures out of my purse and called my family geeks. I mention how he calls me Smelly Nellie. I say, "I only butted him in the head because he tried to look down my shirt while I was bending over and I stood up too fast." By this time my voice is quivering a little.

"It's all right, Nell," Mr. Melnyk says. "I have some idea how Shane acts around girls. I didn't realize things had gone this far, but we'll put an end to it. I promise you that."

By the time I leave Foods for lunch, Shane and Mr. Melnyk are over in a corner. I can't hear much of what's going on, but Mr. Melnyk keeps punching the air with his finger and I'm pretty sure he says, "Zero tolerance!" a couple of times. It's a slogan we hear around the school all the time.

When the noon break begins every day, a group of boys collect in the first floor stair landing and rate the girls who pass by. They've given me nothing out of ten so many times that I hardly ever go to my locker before lunch anymore. Unlike Mr. Melnyk, I have no tolerance for zero at all.

I was the first person out of Foods today, though. There

are only a few people in the hallway and I really do hate lugging books home at noon, so I dash up the stairs for a quick locker visit. Unfortunately, it's not quick enough.

When I come back down the stairs, the boys are gathered in their usual place. I try to scuttle past with my eyes down, but somebody pushes me from behind and they make a closed circle around me. They're all smiling, but not like they're glad to see me.

"Well, well," one of them says, "if it isn't Smelly Nellie." He starts sniffing around me and then the rest of them join in. It makes me uncomfortable in my skin.

"I have to pick up my brother," I say, and try to push my way out. They make the circle tighter. "Let me go!"

"Boys," says a voice I know right away belongs to Shane. "Don't touch that mouse!" I guess I thought he'd be whisked away from school in a windowless van or something, but here he is. So much for his talk with Mr. Melnyk.

Shane's standing on the outside of the circle and away from me. "What you're doing is called harassment, boys," Shane says. "Don't you know we have ZERO TOLERANCE for that at this school?" He leans on the zero.

"No," one of them mumbles, "ZERO TOLERANCE?" Others laugh and repeat the two words, like Shane is Moses and he's just brought down the Ten Commandments.

"We have to let poor Smelly go," Shane says. "We can't harass her at school."

"Can we harass her when she's not at school?" someone asks.

Shane just shrugs, does his claw thing, turns and slouches away. Then the circle opens, the other boys walk away too, and except for the roughness in my stomach, it's just like I imagined the whole thing.

Chapter Two

When I get to Mary Chase School to pick up my little brother, he isn't waiting for me by the side door like he's supposed to be. He's also not in his classroom. Neither is Mrs. Montcrieff, his teacher, so I go to the office.

"I'm Nell Hopkins," I tell the secretary. "I need to pick up my little brother, Mike, and I can't find him. He's in Mrs. Montcrieff's Grade Two class."

She flips through some blue sheets on a clipboard and says, "I'm sorry. I don't see a Mike in that class."

"There has to be one," I say, "I delivered one there this morning."

"You're his sister?" I nod. She looks back to the clipboard. Then she smiles. "You must be looking for Lester B. Hopkins."

"Yes," I say. "I forgot you called him that here."

"It's a very unusual name for a little boy."

She's being nice, so I try to be. "We're an unusual family. My brother is named after Lester B. Pearson, the Prime Minister who put the Maple Leaf on our flag." I don't mention that our mother worships the guy because he won the Nobel Peace Prize before she was even born. I'm still a little shaky, and don't feel like getting into information mode. Now it's the secretary's turn to nod.

"People usually call my little brother Mike, though, just like they did the Prime Minister. I mostly call him Mikey. Do you know where he is?"

"I'm afraid I haven't seen him," she says. "Let me call Mrs. Montcrieff for you."

In a minute, Mikey's teacher is in the office too. "Hello, Nell," she says. "I imagine you're looking for Lester B.?"

Mrs. Montcrieff and my mother are the only two people who can use my little brother's formal name and get away with it. When I call him that, he goes into orbit. "Or Mikey," I say. "Whichever."

Mrs. Montcrieff takes my arm and leads me toward a room with a closed door. A sign on it says "Wellness Room." As she opens the door, she says, "Your brother's been very upset this morning, Nell. I hope you can help me find out what it's about." She gestures for me to go into the room and says, "I'll leave you alone for a moment."

Actually, I'm not very much help at all when Mikey really wigs out. It's my temper again. He can get very emotional – I mean really out of control – and when he does that, I think I get scared. And when I'm scared or embarrassed, I blow up, which generally makes things worse.

I've already had enough trouble today, though, and I'm pressing very hard on my self-control button, but I still get that dangerous, fluttery feeling in my stomach when I look at my little brother. The Wellness Room is a nice buttery yellow, with paintings of sunflowers on the walls. Mikey isn't taking in any of that brightness, though. He's lying in a ball on his side with a flowered quilt tucked around him. His face is very pale, which makes his hair seem even redder, and his eyes are closed. There are tear tracks on his cheeks.

"What's going on, Mikey?" I ask. I sit down on the edge of the bed and pat his back a little, the way our mother would if she was still around.

Mikey rolls over. "She's dead," he says. He opens his eyes. They're soft, and grey, and sensitive – like Mom's. Right away they fill up with tears.

Grey eyes are another thing I don't share with my family. Even Uncle Martin has them. Mine are hazel, speckled with gold. I suppose you could say they're unusual, but I don't know. Especially since I came to JAWS, I don't feel like there's anything special about me.

"Who's dead?" I ask Mikey.

I figure he's reliving the death of Merit, the dog we had when we lived outside of Edmonton, in a little town called Beaumont. That was just last year according to the calendar, but it seems like light years ago to me. As it turns out, I'm wrong.

"Mom," he tells me.

"Mom?" I ask. "Mom? How do you know that? When did you hear?"

"I know," he says. "And she's dead." He blinks, and two

huge tears roll down his cheeks and fall onto the blue-and-white knit collar of his shirt. I took that shirt out of the dryer just this morning. It still has a nice clean smell.

"Mike," I say, "you can't possibly know that for sure." My voice is high and squeaky and I swallow a couple of times. "Uncle Martin would hear first. And I know he'd tell me, too."

Mikey pulls his mouth really tight and scrunches up his eyes. "I know it for sure," he says. "I wouldn't lie."

"Well," I say. "Well." I'm not even sure where to go next. "You still haven't said how you found out."

Mikey gets this glazed look in his eyes. "Emily Carr told me."

Considering the kind of morning I've had, it's not surprising that this pushes me over the edge. Emily Carr is the artist of the month at Mary Chase. She's also been dead for over half a century. "Mike!" I blurt out, "don't be ridiculous! Why do you make up stuff like this, anyway?"

"I'm not making anything up! Emily Carr came to school today, Nellie Lettuce-Head!"

"Excuse me," I say, "WRONG!" My middle name is Letitia, and Lettuce-Head is something Mikey calls me when he's really upset. He thinks it's very clever, and usually laughs afterwards. Today, he doesn't.

"Emily Carr is dead," I say. "And Mom's alive." I try to get my voice back under control. "We've had two e-mails from her in the last four days."

Mikey sits up in bed and I can see he's working up a real

head of steam. "Emily Carr was at school today! Ask Mrs. Montcrieff if you don't believe me!"

Mrs. Montcrieff must have stepped back into the room during my outburst, because now he turns and whines to her, "Emily Carr was here today, wasn't she, Mrs. M.?"

Mrs. Montcrieff smiles and says, "That's true, Lester B., but –"

"I told you," Mikey says and he gives me a very pouty, triumphant look.

My mouth is probably hanging open at this point, because Mrs. Montcrieff goes on, "I think I should say, an actor was here playing the role of Emily Carr."

"Oh," I say, shaking my head. "An actor." Like that makes everything better.

*M*aybe I haven't mentioned that Mary Chase School is a little on the artsy side, and they do weird things like this with the students all the time. I suppose that's okay for average kids, or older ones. If you brought some ghosts into my classes at JAWS, they'd fit in so well with the other dead-heads that I doubt anyone would notice. Or if they did, they certainly wouldn't freak out. "I think that's Emily Carr over there doing the dishes," I might say to Priscilla Wong.

"How do you spell her last name?" Priscilla would probably ask, because she'd want to write it down.

But my little brother can go off the deep end pretty easily, and this kind of thing just mixes him up. I think what he needs is a school where they sit in rows and do worksheets. He'd probably hate it, but it would help him get control of his imagination.

Unfortunately, nobody asked what I thought when we were figuring out schools for the year. Mom wanted Mikey to go to Mary Chase while we're staying with our Uncle Martin, because it's close to his house, and my brother would be able to make friends in the neighbourhood. So far he's made one – Denver, the dog who lives across the street at Mr. Lapinski's – but I suppose that number can change.

Mom also wanted me to go to JAWS because it's close to Mary Chase and I could pick Mikey up and take him home for lunch. Also, walk home with him after school. "It's only until I get back and we're sorted out again," she said before she left. "You can handle it, can't you, Nellie? You don't mind?"

First I told her I didn't want to be called Nellie any more. Then I said, "Yes, I do mind. What about the academic program they don't have at JAWS? What about the choir they don't have? What about the fact that the school is ready to collapse and hasn't been painted in about forty years?"

That last bit was an exaggeration, of course. JAWS – the building – isn't really falling apart, even though it's pretty grungy in some parts. It's more like when you're in it, you've entered some kind of time warp. The main school entrance, for instance, has showcases with glass fronts on either side filled with sports trophies and academic awards. (Also quite a few dead flies.) I suppose the trophies might look impressive at first, but if you look closely, you'll notice that the most recent date on any of them is 1985. That gives you a pretty good idea of what a humming place JAWS is. Mom wasn't picky about that, though.

In the end, Mikey pouted and cried because he wanted me near by. And Uncle Martin, who teaches art in a high school pretty close to the academic junior high I would LIKE to attend, said over and over to my mom, "I just don't know how this is going to work out, Alice. I'd feel better if Nell went to school in the neighbourhood."

And Nell, being me and sometimes fierce on the outside but pretty mushy in the middle, said, "Okay." That's what she said out loud, anyway. But in the head I share with her, what she thought was, "Fine. I'll stay in the neighbourhood and go to JAWS, but don't expect me to be happy about it."

Chapter Three

One good thing about Mary Chase School is Mrs. Montcrieff. She really is a very kind person. She decides that Mikey needs to stay at school for the rest of the day where she can keep an eye on him. Blowing up at me seems to have made him feel better, but Uncle Martin has his Art 30 students out on a field trip for the day and can't be reached, so she's calling the shots.

"What if he gets hungry?" I want to know.

"I'll make him a sandwich in the staff room," Mrs. Montcrieff says. "We always have bread and cheese on hand. You go on home, Nell, have lunch yourself, and come back here when your classes are over at the end of the day. I'm sure by then Lester B. will be able to go home with you."

"I guess," I say. I find my brother very irritating most of the time, but I don't really like walking off and leaving him.

"It's all right," she says, "I'll talk to your uncle this evening. You go on and try not to worry." Then she squeezes my hand and leaves.

When I get home, I make my famous tomato soup lunch, but for one this time instead of two. What I do is put a can of tomato soup in a saucepan with a half-cup of water, and a half-cup of evaporated milk. I heat it slowly so it doesn't burn, and then I add some grated cheese. Mikey doesn't like anything else with it, but Uncle Martin keeps lots of fancy ingredients around, so today I put my soup in a big red-and-white-striped mug, and plop sour cream and chopped candied ginger on top. I make some raisin toast to go with it and put that on a plate, along with a few of those baby carrots you can buy that are peeled and ready to eat.

With all the food preparation and slurping and chewing, plus biting my nails and staring out the window, it's 1:15 before I know it. I'm just thinking what a disappointment it is that I won't be able to make it back to school on time when the phone rings. The answering machine picks up the call and a voice says, "Hello, Mr. and Mrs. Hopkins? This is a parent volunteer in the office of James A. Wyndotte School calling. Your daughter, Nellie Hopkins, is absent from classes this afternoon. Will you please confirm with the school whether or not you are aware of this absence by calling 438-9210? Thank you."

I've been a student at JAWS for almost two months and I think by now someone should have looked at my registration form and noticed that I live with my uncle, Mr. Martin

Mackelwain, and not with my parents. Not with my parent, I should say, since Bob Hopkins, who passes for my father, hasn't been in the picture since Mikey was two years old. The flecks in my eyes and the fly-away hair are just part of what I have against him.

They should also have noticed that I do not like to be called Nellie. "PLEASE CALL ME NELL," I printed across the top of that same form in capital letters and very dark ink. So far, Mr. Melnyk is the only one who's noticed.

I stay at the table for a while, tearing the back page of the JAWS newsletter into little pieces. It's a colour called goldenrod, and I don't care for it very much. I suppose I could go to school late with some excuse or other. But I really don't want to go near the place. When I have a pile of goldenrod paper bits in my soup mug, I finally decide to go for a ride on my bike until Mikey is ready to come home. Bike rides help me clear my head. Sometimes I ride for hours.

Before I leave the house, I erase the message from JAWS on the answering machine. I've always been a very honest person, so it's not something I'd normally do. I don't feel quite like myself these days, though, whatever that is. Part of it is that Uncle Martin's not used to kids my age and he can get very intense. And I don't want to talk to him about personal things. I'm hoping the bike ride will help me think of a way to avoid that permanently.

I go clear out past Gold Bar Park and up onto the bluffs above the North Saskatchewan River. I like it there. You don't see the refineries at all, and it's almost like you're in the wilderness. The leaves are gone from the trees because it's late October, but the sun's shining and the air is really warm. I saw on the weather channel that it's the warmest autumn in northern Alberta since they've kept records of such things.

I have a whole bench all to myself, so I sit down and try to decide what I should do about the various messes I seem to be in. Maybe you figure I should just tell my uncle about everything when he gets home tonight and let him handle it. I am a kid, after all. I'm not supposed to have all the answers. But here's what I mean about the way he acts.

Just before Mom left, the four of us spent a few days together in Edmonton. We'd packed up our house in Beaumont, put some of our stuff in storage, and moved the rest into Uncle Martin's house. Both he and my mother are really into folk music, so one day we went into the river valley for the Folk Festival.

We put up our tent on the hill that overlooks the main stage in Gallagher Park. It was a sunny day and the mosquitoes weren't trying to make off with anybody. We had pop and lemonade in a cooler and these special folding chairs to sit on.

It started out to be a real flag-waving Canadian day. We heard Connie Kaldor sing about the Saskatchewan prairie first, and then somebody we'd never heard of went on for a while about the way the wind blows in Alberta. Not long after that, two women came on stage. Mikey was jabbering away about something and Uncle Martin shushed him.

"It's Kate and Anna McGarrigle," he said. Since he wasn't announcing the arrival of Elmo or some other bigwig in my brother's Grade Two world, Mikey quieted down a little but went on talking. "They're from down East," Uncle Martin added. For some odd reason, that seemed to do the trick, and Mikey was suddenly very attentive.

"Actually, Martin, they're from Montreal," Mom said.

"They really sound like it," I chimed in. I just couldn't resist saying that. Uncle Martin shushed us again, but no one was upset. It was just minor haggling and nothing to get excited about.

When the McGarrigles finished, Uncle Martin went to the refreshment shacks and brought back kielbasa on kaiser rolls for all of us. He piled a lot of sauerkraut on them, the way he likes. Mikey, of course, got in a snit and wouldn't eat his.

"It's only sauerkraut, Mike," Uncle Martin said, looking a little offended. Maybe he thought having a name for the stringy stuff all over Mikey's kielbasa would settle him down. But Mikey started shrieking and wailing. "No! No! It stinks! Get it off!"

"Look," Uncle Martin said, "it's delicious." He held up a long string of sauerkraut, tipped his head back and made a big show of gobbling it down.

"I hate it!" Mikey moaned. He dropped his paper plate down on the ground and the kielbasa rolled out of the bun and onto the grass. Then he started crying, "My lunch! I'm hungry!" Stuff like that.

"Mike!" Uncle Martin snapped, and he moved toward my little brother, I suppose homing in on the idea that he needed a stern, male authority figure to sort him out. But Mom shot in front of him, picked up Mikey's kielbasa, used her fingers to rake off the strings of sauerkraut that still clung to it, put the sausage – by now looking pretty stressed out – back into its bun, and handed it to Mikey.

Uncle Martin just kind of stopped in mid-stride with his mouth open, then went back and sat down. He tried to look like he wasn't annoyed, but being a redhead, his face was flaming by then. And his square Mackelwain jaw stuck out farther than usual, which is saying a lot. (No, I don't have the family jaw either, although it's possible it may develop later on.)

Mikey started eating, and a new group came up on stage – gospel singers from Georgia, I think, or maybe Tennessee. We all listened like we were thinking about becoming gospel singers ourselves and needed to get all the tips we could in a hurry.

Then I heard Mom say quietly, "It's not a food he's familiar with, Martin. That's all. I don't think we need to make an issue of it."

Uncle Martin sighed. "Well," he said, "I'm so fond of it myself, I didn't think." My mom is his big sister, after all, and I guess he's used to her being right, but that still doesn't mean he likes it.

In a little while he turned to her and in his own version of a quiet voice, which is low and kind of raspy, said, "Sauerkraut has amazing nutritional properties, Aly. I can't understand why you haven't introduced it to your children." Mom just looked at him, held her nose, and shivered.

*T*hat was the end of the kielbasa episode, but food is still an issue between Mikey and Uncle Martin. He eats lots of other painful and disgusting stuff like one hundred-year-old eggs and hot food from Indonesia that leaves scorched places in my throat as big as SOS pads. Mikey starts yelling as soon as he sees the little bottles of chilies and other spices Uncle Martin uses to create these terrible dishes.

I guess what I'm really saying is that Uncle Martin seems prissy and a bit weird to me. And it isn't just because of his diet. He insists that we listen to certain kinds of music while we eat, depending on what he's cooking. If it's Italian, we hear opera. If it's Chinese, we hear low voices groaning like their owners have major cases of food poisoning, while gongs and temple bells ring in the background. I wouldn't complain too much if we listened to some old stuff like the Beatles, but Uncle Martin reserves their music for when he's in the shower. "Let It Be" is his favourite. It's really something to wake up on a school morning and hear him singing that in the bathroom.

I know Uncle Martin has a right to eat anything and

listen to anything he wants to in his own house. And it probably isn't fair to expect him to know how to act around kids our age. The ones he teaches in high school are older and, I guess, very serious about painting, or tearing pictures out of magazines and pasting them down on paper.

I do appreciate the fact that he's letting us stay with him while Mom is gone. I'm trying to, at least. But I also don't think it's fair to expect us to live with a MAN of any size or shape when we're not used to it – especially one who leaves long, red hairs in the bathtub drain, and has food and music fetishes. And there's just no way I'm going talk to him about private stuff.

I said more to Mr. Melnyk than I was comfortable with because Shane drove me to it, but it's really the kind of thing I'd like to talk to my mother about – if she was here, that is. I've already told you she isn't. And though I don't really like saying this out loud, I'm not even technically sure she's mine at the moment. Or that Mikey isn't right and we'll never see her again. That really shakes me up.

Chapter Four

*T*his is the way my park bench thinking is turning out. It isn't helping me very much, so I stretch out on the bench with my puffy red ski vest under my head and close my eyes. The sun feels good on my face and I start to relax a little. I'm wondering if Mikey's still in his little cocoon at Mary Chase, or if he's gone back to class, when suddenly it comes to me that I can solve his problem very easily without involving Uncle Martin at all. That way, if he finds out that I didn't go to school this afternoon, he'll see it was for a very good reason. He'll be so happy I've relieved him of Mikey's problem that he'll write me an excuse and we won't have to talk about personal stuff at all.

What I'll do is, I'll get the name of the actress who impersonated Emily Carr from Mrs. Montcrieff. Then I'll call her as soon as Mikey and I get home. If I'm lucky, which I admit I haven't been lately, she'll be home and I'll be able to get the real story out of her. I can be very tough when I need to be.

After I have this mental breakthrough, I obviously fall

asleep, because the next thing I know, I'm looking at my watch and noticing that it's three o'clock and I only have half an hour to get back to Mary Chase. I jump on my bike and pedal off like crazy. Most of the way I'm going downhill and I can speed along, but eventually I have to get up out of the river valley.

I usually follow the main bike path that winds up gradually, but that takes me about six blocks too far west. Since I'm in a hurry, I decide to use a much steeper walking trail that goes straight up the bluff and brings me out in front of the Highlands Senior Citizen Centre, and about two blocks from Mikey's school. I'll have to push my bike up the wooden steps at the top – maybe eight dozen of them – but I figure I can handle it. I've got great legs, like I said, and I'm not afraid of a little exercise.

Even so, I'm pretty winded by the time I'm near the top. I've just decided to rest for a while, when I hear a horn honking and kids yelling somewhere up above. I move cautiously up the last few steps and stop in the cover of some bushes. A minivan is trying to pull away from the curb in front of the Highlands Centre. Three guys have stretched their arms out and made a line across the street in front of it, so the van can't move forward without mowing one of them down. The driver leans on the horn.

"Be polite!" one of the guys yells.

"Yeah! What's the magic word?" another one taunts. They all laugh and look at each other.

The one farthest from me claws at the air with both hands. There's no doubt where I've seen that before.

The van driver rolls down the window. "I have elderly people in here, and some have medical conditions," he snaps. "Move or I'll phone the police!"

A car pulls in behind the van, and then a pick-up truck pulls in behind the car. Both drivers lay on the horn. Also, a bunch of people have come out of the Centre. One white-haired lady in a plaid coat calls out, "The police are on their way!"

An old man shakes his finger at the kids and shouts, "What's the matter with you young folks? Don't you have any respect?"

"Okay, Grandpa, keep your shirt on," Shane yells back. He turns around and begins slouching down the street toward me. I go into a deep crouch as a second guy follows him. The third doesn't budge, though, and there's not quite enough room for the vehicles to go around him.

Anyway, this final guy takes out a cigarette and lights up. Then as he turns around toward me, he blows out a big show-off puff of smoke – like being in love with nicotine makes him a hero, instead of an idiot. That's when he pushes back his sweatshirt hood and I get a glimpse of raggedly cut hair streaked with red and black. That's also when I realize he's not a guy, at all! He's a really tall GIRL, with lots of black eye makeup, and a couple of rings in her lower lip.

Cars are honking at her, people are shouting, but she just swaggers slowly away with this wreath of smoke around her head. I get the feeling she loves being in the middle of all that commotion.

Chapter Five

I have to make sure Shane and his friends are gone before I come up out of the ravine, so it's 3:26 when I skid into the Mary Chase parking lot. I lock up my bike and go into the school. In four more minutes the hall will be full of kids.

As it turns out, I don't need to ask anybody for Emily Carr's phone number, because there she is, all by herself, walking toward me. Uncle Martin brought home a book about her when he found out Mikey was studying her painting at school. I helped my brother read it. Now, I couldn't miss her if I tried.

She's short and stout, wearing a paint-spattered white smock over a long skirt. She's pushing a doll carriage full of artist supplies and toy dogs, and she has a stuffed monkey wrapped around her neck. There's this black hairnet thing pulled down over her head.

The real Emily Carr did push her painting supplies around in a baby carriage, although the English sheepdogs she raised wouldn't have fit into it unless they were puppies.

But the toy monkey looks a lot like the real one Emily kept as a pet. I can't remember its name.

I surprise myself by walking right up to her. "I need to ask you something," I say.

"Of course, my dear," she says. She's got a Scottish accent, and her voice is quite low and marmeladey.

I'm careful not to forget my manners. "Ma'am," I say, "you told my little brother something this morning that scared him witless. I don't think that was right."

"Did I?" she asks. "I'm terribly sorry."

I tell her how Mikey thinks he heard her say our mother is dead, and even though I'm pretty sure she's alive – at least she was yesterday – he won't believe me. I say that he's been curled up in a ball in the Wellness Room all day because he's so wigged out about it.

She looks really sad and keeps saying "Oh dear" under her breath. Eventually she takes my hand. Then it's like I can't stop talking. For the second time today, I blab on about all kinds of personal stuff. I'm about to go into detail about Shane and his friends, when several classroom doors open at the same time and the hall is suddenly filled with kids.

They press all around us calling her name. They touch her clothes and pet the monkey's tail. "Oh, Emily," says one little girl with braces and about six ponytails sticking out all over her head. "Will you be back tomorrow?"

"I don't expect so, dear," Emily says. "It's very tiring being around so many young people when you're normally . . . resting."

"But you like us, don't you?" asks another little girl with butterfly clips in her dark hair and skin the colour of creamy coffee. "You like it at our school?"

"I absolutely love it," Emily answers. "It's been a wonderful day for me, but after all, I'm over a hundred years old and I have to look after myself."

"Poor Emily," say several kids at once. A little boy with a buzz cut asks if he can get her some pop. The butterfly girl says, "It's tea. She's meant to drink tea and have cucumber sandwiches. That's what Mrs. del Rio said." (She's the art teacher. Uncle Martin has met her and is over the top about her art program.)

"Yes," says Emily. "Tea and sandwiches." She looks at me, kind of winks, and shrugs her shoulders. "You wouldn't believe how many years it's been since I've had a proper tea. Why don't you children find Mrs. del Rio for me and tell her that I'm ready for refreshment?"

After the girls leave, we're alone again. The Emily Carr impersonator turns to me and asks, very quietly, "Where is your brother now?" I tell her he was in the Wellness Room when I left. "Let me finish up," she says. "Then I'll meet you and your little brother there." I nod, but I think I must look a little unsure because she says again, "Really. I'll come just as soon as I can. Give me fifteen minutes, tops."

I'm just standing there, looking at her, when the same kids come bustling back again with about a dozen others. Some of them take Emily's hand, others push the carriage, and they lead her down the hallway, chattering away. "It's tea time! Come with us, Emily. It's time for tea!"

"How wonderful," Emily says. She looks over her shoulder at me again. "Help, at last!"

As they walk down the hall, I hear her voice rising and falling, telling the children how she wishes she'd had their help when she was taking in lodgers in Victoria. I know the story. It was during World War I and she was so poor she had to rent out rooms in her house and cook for the people who stayed in them. Her boarders didn't like the way she painted, though. They claimed they couldn't eat in the dining room unless she took her pictures down. "Go ahead and starve, then," I would have said. But Emily Carr was the one in danger of starving, so she put all her pictures in the attic and left them there for a lot of years. Being a loner myself, I think I understand how she felt.

I stand there for another minute or two feeling like – I don't know. Just feeling. Then I go looking for Mikey. I find him stretched out on the Wellness Room bed, reading one of the books Mom gave him before she left. Somebody's brought him a fluffy blanket, which he has across his legs, and there's a stuffed pig tucked into the crook of his left arm. Now I'm really convinced that's he's made up the whole thing just to get attention.

"Hi, Mikey. How are things?" I ask.

"Okay," he says, "but I want to go home."

"Let's go then," I say, and I pick up his backpack, which Mrs. Montcrieff has obviously brought to him. It's about half Mikey's height, blue and red and yellow, with lots of flaps and pockets. On one flap there's a white dog bone with "Clifford" on it and a row of fire hydrants underneath. On a zippered pocket below that, a big red dog smiles and waves his paw against a plaid background. Putting the two together, you probably already know it's a picture of Clifford the Big Red Dog. For some unknown reason, he's my brother's favourite fictional character.

"I don't mean go home to Uncle Martin's house," he says. "I mean really home. To our Beaumont home. I want to go back there."

I sit down beside him on the bed and hold the backpack in my lap. "We can't go there, Mikey," I say in the flattest voice I can muster. "It isn't our house any more. We were just renting it and now someone else is living there. We have to stay with Uncle Martin until our mother gets home."

Now Mikey's face crumples up and we go through pretty much the same thing as we did in the morning. "But she's dead," he wails. He takes his time crying, and I'm at the place where I'm ready to surrender, if I could just find out where to go to do that, when the door opens and Emily Carr comes into the room with Mrs. Montcrieff behind her. Mikey stares like he's seen a ghost. Then he unloads.

"It's you!" he wails. "You said that our mother is dead! I heard you! Tell my sister what you said! Please!"

Emily Carr, who Mrs. Montcrieff tells us is really an

actor named Christine Stuart, takes off the black hairnet and runs her hands through her hair. It's short like mine and shot through with white streaks which probably come from a bottle, because even though she has little lines at the corners of her eyes and around her mouth, she doesn't seem that old.

She sighs and looks at Mikey the same sad way she looked at me. "Lester B.," she says (that makes three people who now call him by his real name), "I'm so sorry. I have no idea what I said that made you think your mother is dead, but she's fine. Everyone says so." I nod. Mrs. Montcrieff nods, even though we don't know for sure what we're talking about.

Mikey throws the stuffed pig on the floor. He rolls his head and flutter kicks his legs up and down on the cot. "You said it!" he wails. "I heard you say it! My mother is dead! Alice is dead!" I could cheerfully smack him for making such a scene.

"What did I say, exactly?" asks Emily-who's-turned-out-to-be-Christine. She puts her hands on her knees and leans forward.

Mikey is quiet for a minute, like he's run out of steam. He looks up at the ceiling. Finally he says in a whisper, "You said some person is dead. She's up in heaven with Alice! That's my mother, isn't it?" He looks at me and his eyes are open really wide. "Our mother is Alice, isn't she, Nellie?"

"Sure, Mike," I say, "but there must be lots of –"

"I know what I said now!" Christine says. She snaps her

fingers and holds up her arms like she's ready to sing, or say hallelujah. "I was standing in the hall at recess. A little girl came up to me and told me that her grandmother had just died. She asked me if I knew where she was now. I said, 'I'm sure she must be in heaven, with Alice and me. I'll look her up when I get back.' Alice is the name of Emily Carr's sister. When Emily Carr died in 1945, she was living with her sister, Alice. I didn't mean your mother."

Mikey looks at me again. "But our mother's name is Alice. And you said she was dead." He goes on sniffling and shaking his head.

"I meant Alice Carr, son," says Christine. "I had no idea you might think I meant your mother. I'm terribly sorry." She looks at Mrs. Montcrieff like she needs reassurance.

Mrs. Montcrieff pulls this little stool over beside the bed and sits down. "You must have been very frightened, Lester B.," she says. She picks up the pig and tucks it back under his arm. Then she pats down his hair where it's sticking up at the back. He looks at her out of the corner of his eyes and nods. He sighs.

"I thought me and Nellie were all alone," he says. "Except for Uncle Martin, and his house smells funny."

"He just cooks weird stuff," I say to both women. "Right now he's making sauerkraut. From scratch, I mean." They both nod and smile, like living with someone who makes their own sauerkraut is something they have also experienced and lived through.

I reach out my hand to Mikey – I'm just thinking I'll

pat his back again, but he slides right over and crawls onto my lap. Am I amazed! I put my arms around him and hold him while Mrs. Montcrieff and Christine tell him what a little champ he's turning out to be to live so bravely without his mother. Then I embarrass myself – again – by choking up. I do it quietly and into the back of Mikey's neck, but I'm sure they can hear me snivelling all the same.

Chapter Six

Mikey's different than I am. I mean, he's worried about our mother. But he's not angry at her for taking off the way I am. As far as he's concerned, she's a saint. He's put up pictures of her all around Uncle Martin's spare bedroom where he's sleeping now: Mom doing the laundry. Mom and Merit out in the yard. Mom and Mikey and Merit out in the yard. Mom in her combat gear. Mom holding her C-7 rifle and smiling. Mom waving from the window of a huge truck.

I've been avoiding saying it, but she's a non-commissioned officer in the Canadian Reserve. I'd rather not say it even now, but it happens to be the truth. Along with around six hundred other people from the battalion in Edmonton, my mother, Master Corporal Alice S. Mackelwain, is a peacekeeper, running around in Bosnia, doing what she calls "stabilization work." What I call it is trying to make other families happy and safe instead of looking after her own.

At first when Mikey blurted out that Mom was dead, I thought he'd heard something and that she really had been killed. I wasn't using my head, of course. Army brass wouldn't call a seven-year-old boy at school to tell him his mother had ... you know.

Maybe you think I'm overreacting. I know it's supposed to be pretty safe in Bosnia now, compared to how it was when the first peacekeepers arrived about five years ago. Mom's always going on about that in her e-mails – Mikey has saved them all in a special file. It's pretty much a ritual that when he gets home from school, he turns on the computer, reads over his favourite letters, and then writes back.

I thought he might be too tired today, but he isn't. I can hear him reading out loud while I'm in the kitchen, micro-waving popcorn for a snack. He stumbles and puzzles over some of the words, but he's a pretty good reader and gets most of them right. That's actually saying a lot, because Mom doesn't use easy words just because she's writing to her own children.

Unfortunately, Mikey always reads the headings and closings with all their numbers and squiggles. And that's starting to get monotonous.

"What do you call the sideways v-things on both ends of Mom's e-mail address?" he asked me when her first letter came.

"Sideways v-things, I guess," I told him. "Why?"

"I think they look like crocodile jaws," he said. So that's

how he reads Mom's address now. "Crocodile mail466 @dnd.ca crocodile."

*I*ve read our mother's letters almost as much as Mikey has, of course, even though I'm upset with her for leaving and I'm not writing back. From the sound of it, right now he's reading the one about the lady who chains up her cow. He really likes it. I think it's the first letter we got.

Subject:	**Greetings from Bosnia**
Date:	September 15, 2000 20:20:01
From:	"MCpl.AS.Mackelwain,ASU Edmonton, 582-5418,0900" <mail466@dnd.ca>
To:	mmackelwain@hotmail.com

Dear Nell and Lester B.,

We've arrived at Grey Wolf, our camp near the village of Velika Kladusa, and are settled in. The countryside around here is hilly and green and there are lots of pine trees. From a distance it doesn't look like there's been a war, although in the cities and towns it's another matter.

I've got a little trailer to stay in. It's called an ISO, and the whole thing flattens down so it can be moved. It has one window and a door. My roommate's name is Lorna Karlsen. We each have a single bed, a locker, a hardback chair, and a lamp. Lorna's a radio operator and she usually works different hours than I do, so we are managing to share the space without much trouble.

I don't have any complaints about the food in the mess where we eat. They always have omelets available for breakfast, lunch, and dinner, and if I don't like the look of what they're serving, I have one of those. The bread is excellent! Every day a truck loaded with it arrives from a bakery in V.K. at about 05:00 – that's five o'clock a.m. in civilian time.

Everyone loves the sweet rolls the baker makes. They're a little like doughnuts on the outside, with chocolate pudding in the middle. People who have night gate duty think they're pretty lucky because they get to end their shift with hot bread and rolls before anyone else is really awake.

Today is my day off and I'm going to spend it visiting an elderly woman named Bojana Cikic. She lives in a two-room house about thirty minutes away from Grey Wolf. She's one of the people the Red Cross has been alerted to look after because she needs fresh water and food. They are prepared to help her if she comes to their camp, but they don't have the number of transport vehicles required to make visits to people in outlying areas. And she won't leave her house because there are still land mines all around it. There's a de-mined path from the road to her front door. We use it for our visits, but we can't convince Bojana to use it as well. Can you imagine what it would be like to have only one safe way in and out of your Uncle Martin's house in Edmonton?

We take Bojana fresh water twice a week, and when we go, we ask the kitchen for two box lunches. There are four sandwiches, two pieces of fruit, and a drink box in each lunch. We make sure we've had a good breakfast and then leave everything with her. The food and water we bring is mostly what she survives on. It isn't a lot, but it's something we can do that doesn't involve miles of red tape. I wish we could do more.

I know you're both worried about the land mine situation here, but I want to tell you again that it's perfectly safe going to her house as long as we stay on the marked pathway. She's just shaken by the war and doesn't always trust what we tell her.

On our way home we're going to visit another woman whose name is Irena Martinovic. Most of her family either died in the war or are still listed as missing. She and her husband struggle to grow food on the small section of their land that has been cleared of bombs. They have two apple trees and a little patch of garden. It's dormant now, except for some winter squash and onions. They also have a cow.

In Canada, we fence in huge fields for our cattle to graze, but we keep our dogs in the house or tied up. Here it's the reverse. Dogs run everywhere, but Irena's cow is so important to her survival that she puts chains around its horns and tethers it to a tree to keep it from wandering off and getting blown up.

The thing that amazes me about her is that she's

always cheerful, and despite the fact that she doesn't have much, she insists on giving us something when any of us stop by. Once she gave me some knitted slippers. And she makes coffee for us that's so thick you can practically eat it with a spoon. She serves it really sweet, in little doll-sized cups.

It's night now and I need to get some sleep. Tomorrow I have to make the two-hour drive up to Zagreb to pick up a shipment of supplies and bring it back here. I'll be driving in a convoy of eight or ten vehicles. None of us have any idea whether we'll be transporting important items like antibiotics or powdered milk, or something less essential. Last week I drove all the way down with a load of toilet paper. Whatever they give me is what I take.

Someone else is waiting to use the computer, so I'd better go. I haven't heard anything from either of you yet, but I'm sure I will any day. It can't be too soon for me.

Love you and miss you,

Mom
"MCpl.AS.Mackelwain,ASU Edmonton,582-5418,0900"
e-mail:466@dnd.ca

Can you see what I mean? She wants us to know that it's perfectly safe in Bosnia as long as you don't step on a mine. But I've been checking this out on the Internet and I've learned that there are between three and six million land mines still uncleared in that country, so stepping on one isn't exactly hard to do. And our mom travels all the time. That's what she does. She drives this big truck all over the country delivering food and medical supplies. Sometimes she takes people around in a jeep.

She's told us over and over that peacekeepers have maps with orange and red dots on them showing where known land mines are. But of course they're only known because someone remembers where they are and has reported them. It doesn't take a rocket scientist to figure out that there are mines all over the place that people have forgotten about, just like our dog, Merit, used to forget about bones she'd buried in the back yard.

Thinking about this makes me so agitated I rip open the microwave popcorn bag the wrong way. The steam from it burns my wrist, and I rub a little honey on it to take away the sting. Then I put the popcorn into bowls. Mikey and I used to eat directly out of the bag, so that shows how living with Uncle Martin has changed our lifestyle.

I take Mikey's bowl into the computer room, then go back to the kitchen, sit down at the table, and open my library book. Not long after that Mikey comes in carrying his empty bowl. "Is there any more popcorn?" he asks.

"A little," I say, keeping my nose in my book. Both Mikey and Uncle Martin seem to be getting the idea that I like waiting on them, which I don't. "Look in the bag."

Mikey helps himself to more. In fact he helps himself to

all that's left. "Mike," I say. "What about me, please?"

"Sorry," he says. He walks over to me, takes about four kernels out of his bowl and puts them in mine. It's a start, I guess, and I don't want to rock the boat after the day we've had. I'm not very hungry anyway.

"Did you hear me reading?" he asks.

"Do owls have ears?" I answer back.

He takes that as a yes. "Now I'm going to read the one that came yesterday."

"Okay," I say, going back over the sentence I've been stuck on for about five minutes now.

"The one about the little boy with the orange jacket."

"Okay."

"And about Elvis."

"Okay."

"I'm sorry I made a big stink at school today," Mikey says. I look at him then and think how much his eyes are like our mom's. Hers always used to settle me.

I let out a big sigh and sort of pat his shoulder. "You were probably scared." He leans into me. "But you don't have to worry. Mom's okay."

"Okay," he says back. "And after I'm done reading, I'm going to write her about my costume and stuff. I'll tell her Uncle Martin and I are going to finish the Clifford costume tonight." He gives me four more popcorn kernels, then takes the rest and goes off to the computer again. When he's gone, I decide to give up on the book and listen to him read instead.

Subject:	**Elvis is in Bosnia!**
Date:	October 29, 2000 18:45:01 – 10:45:01 (EST)
From:	"MCpl.AS.Mackelwain,ASU Edmonton, 582-5418,0900" <mail466@dnd.ca>
To:	mmackelwain@hotmail.com

Dear Nell and Lester B.,

This is my second e-mail to you in the last few days. They're starting to do some work on the connection, though, so our e-mail may not be very reliable for the next while. Don't worry if you don't hear from me off and on. I'm safe and well.

I've been writing you that on our days off many of us are fixing up the Zijad Setkic grade school near V. K. It has one room and an outdoor toilet, but has been in very bad condition. I think at one point during the war some people sheltered there and they tore up floorboards and stripped wood from the walls to burn in the stove. The village had started using it as a school again, but students were sitting in water puddles and it was cold and unsanitary.

We've fixed the floor and put a new roof on it. We've also put in a new stove and built a new outhouse. We've been given money for some of the repairs, but we took up a collection for the rest. Today we're painting the walls a nondescript beige. It's not exciting, but it's what we could get and it's better than nothing at all.

Every time we drive to the school in our white vans, the kids come out and follow us. There are so many that Lorna, my roommate, and another woman come along when they can just to play games with the children and keep them from getting in the way of the work. Most of the children are young enough to have been born after the hostilities ended here. But a few remember.

One little boy always comes out and watches us. He's a few years younger than you are, Lester B., and he's very shy. He always wears an orange jacket and pants made out of some kind of synthetic fabric that crinkles when he walks. But he has no toque or mitts. He doesn't wear socks and his shoes are thin sandals. It will be hard for him when the weather turns cold.

So far he won't come near anyone but Lorna. He holds his hand out to her and she gives him orange sections or raisins. Yesterday she gave him a chocolate kiss wrapped in silver paper and he smiled at her for the first time.

A man from the village of V.K. has been going with us to act as translator. He also has clearance to come and go on the base. He doesn't sing or play the guitar, but his name is Elvis, anyway. We aren't allowed to go into the village except on official business, so he sometimes goes to town for us when we need certain items. He's also very good at fixing things that break down.

This is a lengthy way of saying that Elvis told all the children in the village that we'd like to visit them at school on Tuesday and bring them some special treats for Halloween.

Speaking of that, I realize I haven't asked either of you

if you've decided what you're going to be this year. The old costumes are in the trunk down in Martin's basement. You probably don't want to be a pirate again, Lester B., but no one at Mary Chase will have seen the costume.

Nell, I haven't heard anything from you since I left. Is something wrong? Are you going to the school dance? What costume are you going to wear?

Love,

Mom
"MCpl.AS.Mackelwain,ASU Edmonton,582-5418,0900"
e-mail:466@dnd.ca

Now that you're getting to know my mom, you probably think I'm a brat for not writing to her and for making her worry. And maybe you think I don't care about anybody in the world but myself. I do, though. I feel rotten hearing that a little kid who's shy and has probably been through a lot might be cold or hungry. Who wouldn't? And I know that what my mom and other peacekeepers are doing in Bosnia is important.

It's just that I keep imagining my mother driving this truck of hers somewhere. I think, what if she feels sick and needs to stop along the road for a minute? She believes she's in a safe area and she needs fresh air, so maybe she opens the door and gets out. Then she stumbles and steps just ten centimetres over the edge of the path. In those ten centimetres is part of a land mine. That's all it will take.

After that I imagine us all sitting around in the living room. "Mikey," I say. "You were right about Mom, after all. She's dead."

"I guess you'll be here permanently," Uncle Martin says. He doesn't look very happy about it. Mikey starts to cry and can't stop. But I just sit and stare and clench my teeth because I'm the first child she ever had and I didn't want to share her with the world.

Chapter Seven

*B*efore she left, our mother assured us we'd be able to call her in Bosnia. This is how it's supposed to work:

You dial area code 613, then a bunch of other numbers. An operator answers and says, *"Bonjour.* Hello."

Then you say, "Trunk number 2780, please."

The operator asks, "That is V.K. in Bosnia?"

You say, "Yes, I know." At that point you think you're about to be successful. Then you get the next question.

"What is the purpose of your call?"

There isn't any way you can make it sound like national defence business, but you go on. "Uh ... my little brother just wants to tell our mother good night. Maybe find out if she's still alive." That's when the operator disconnects.

Mikey and I have tried this a bunch of times. Only once did we get through to V.K. Maybe that operator was somebody's mother, because she told us she wasn't supposed to connect personal calls. She said she'd do it just this once, since we were children. Mom was out somewhere driving toilet paper or party hats around, though, so Mikey still didn't get to talk to her.

She can phone us, of course. She gets three free, fifteen-minute calls a week. But she has to sign up for them ahead of time, and since most people are from the same time zone, the good spots fill up pretty fast.

E-mail is really the best way to get through to her, even if it doesn't work right all the time. When I hear Mikey pecking at the keys, I figure that's what he's doing. And even though I'm feeling tired, I try to gear myself up to making something happen about dinner. Uncle Martin will be late because of the field trip, and I figure if I get everything ready, things will go more smoothly tonight. Then he won't freak out when Mrs. Montcrieff calls him. And he'll forget to ask me how my day went.

Macaroni and cheese is a pretty safe bet for dinner. Mikey likes the way I make it from scratch, so he'll be okay with it. And Uncle Martin will eat it as long as we've got salsa that he can pour all over the top. I'll also make a salad so it looks like I'm paying attention to the Canada Food Guide. Of course, we have to have dessert, so I search the cupboards for a brownie mix. I put that all together and throw it into the oven.

Once I get dinner going, I set the table with placemats and real napkins. I think about putting on some music Uncle Martin will like, but get stuck for a while on what's appropriate for macaroni and cheese. Would it be English because of the cheddar cheese, or Italian because of the pasta? It could even be Chinese, I suppose. I think I read somewhere that the Chinese actually invented pasta in some dynasty or other.

Finally I decide to set a new precedent, and put on a disc the Mason Middle School choir from Beaumont made last year. I sing along with it, and really rev up the descant on "Farewell to Nova Scotia," something I wasn't allowed to do when we made the recording.

By the time Uncle Martin comes in the door, we're halfway through "Blow the Man Down." I'm just taking the macaroni and cheese out of the oven, and it's bubbly and nice and brown on the top. The table is set. Mikey is washing his hands at the kitchen sink and acting very mellow, and I think we almost do – blow Uncle Martin down and away, I mean.

"Well, Nell," he says, with a little smile in his eyes, "this is very pleasant. Just let me get cleaned up." He puts away his briefcase and in a minute comes back, drying his hands. We all sit down to dinner.

I've put the casserole of macaroni and cheese on a hot plate by Uncle Martin's place. That way he can serve everybody, which I figure will make him feel important. It seems to. He doles out the food like it's Christmas and he's Bob Cratchit. He makes soft little appreciative noises as he takes his first bite. "This is good, Nell," he says. I'm counting on his inexperience with children to keep him from suspecting a set-up.

Mikey gives me a little nod, suddenly very polite and mature, and says, "You're a good cook, Nell. I like this food." Then there's just the sound of spoons and forks clicking on plates for a while – people swallowing and saying "Mmm" a few times. Maybe a "Would you pass the...?" or a "Thank you," all nice and civilized.

*U*ncle Martin has done a lot of work on his little house. And I actually like the kitchen a lot. The walls are painted a really pale cream and the countertops and floor are the kind of tile that's the colour of flowerpots – terra cotta, I think it's called. And by the dining room table, French doors open out to a patio. We've got three jack-o'-lanterns on top of the fence posts in the back yard. Mikey and I carved them yesterday and he insisted on putting them outside, even though Halloween isn't until tomorrow. They aren't lit tonight, but the street light is on, and from my place at the table I can clearly see their orangeness against Uncle Martin's mustard-coloured fence.

Of course there are pictures all around the table where we're eating. Most are originals, painted by my uncle's artsy friends. But there's a print of Emily Carr's opposite to where I'm sitting. (I'm talking about the real Emily Carr now. The one who's dead and buried and considerate enough to stay that way.) It's that painting of a tall, thin tree standing all alone in a patch of forest that's been logged off. The title is *Beloved of Heaven and Despised by Earth*. Something like that. It kind of reminds me of my life, if you take out the part about heaven.

After a bit, Mikey announces that it's time for Clifford on TV and asks if he can be excused. He's already had two helpings of macaroni and cheese. And Uncle Martin probably doesn't want to interrupt this rare, peaceful moment in his life by hassling his nephew about a serving of salad, so he says okay. Mikey goes down to the basement, where Uncle Martin keeps the TV. The brownies are still in a pan at the back of the stove, but he's apparently forgotten about them. I never thought I'd live to see that.

I figure I'd better use the moment wisely, so I tell Uncle Martin about the Emily Carr episode. Just as I'm finishing, we get the first of the phone calls. It's Mrs. Montcrieff. Uncle Martin has a cordless phone, which he keeps on the charger in the living room during the day. He goes in there to answer it and doesn't come back to the kitchen until he's finished. "Your brother's all right now, isn't he?" Uncle Martin asks. He sits back down at the table and looks at me for reassurance.

I shrug my shoulders. "Seems like it," I say.

"Still." Uncle Martin clicks the phone on and off a few times, then sets it down on the table. "You know, Nell," he says, "I was opposed to your mother going off on this . . . peacekeeping venture." He pushes himself away from the table and stretches out his long legs.

I nod. How could I not know that? I heard them arguing about it several times, once after we came back from the Folk Festival. Mom was tucking me into bed and talking to me about how bad things had been in Bosnia. She said that even though a lot of Bosnian men were executed, what happened to the women and children was almost worse. Especially the women and young girls. She told me what the Serb and Croat soldiers did to them and said she had to do something to make things better for the ones who survived and for their children.

Like I say, Uncle Martin overheard us talking, and after Mom left me in the bedroom, I heard him giving her the gears about it. "Alice," he said, "are you out of your mind? Nell is a thirteen-year-old girl. I can't believe you're putting pictures like that in her head."

"I hope that's not what I'm doing," Mom said. "But I feel she needs to know that I wouldn't leave her and Lester B. except for some absolutely compelling reason."

"When you use words like *murder* and *rape*, you don't think she gets images of that? You don't think she'll carry them around with her?"

That's what I overheard, so I don't have much doubt about how he feels. "I think your mother's place is here, with you and your brother," Uncle Martin says to me now. "It's not that I don't want you with me. But as I'm sure you've noticed, I don't have any experience as a parent. And what I remember from my childhood isn't very helpful."

"It's only for six months," I say, although I don't know why on earth I'm defending my mother. "Her rotation will be over the beginning of April. And she'll be home for Christmas."

The phone rings again and Uncle Martin picks it up. "Hello," he says. Then, "Just a minute," and hands it to me.

"Me?" I mouth the word silently.

"Aren't you Nellie Hopkins?"

"Unfortunately." I take the phone. "Hello?" No one says anything back, and after a minute I hear a click. I just sit there.

"Problem?" Uncle Martin asks.

I have all kinds of emotions churning around inside, but all I say is, "No one was there." Then I hand him back the phone.

He clicks it off, then looks at me, and I imagine he's trying to think up what to say next when it rings again. He's still holding it, and he jumps. "Yes," he says, kind of sternly. Then he's silent for a moment. After that he says, "Of course," and "Oh, yes," a bunch of times. He nods and kind of smiles. Pretty soon he goes back into the living room, but I can still hear him going on and on in this odd, throaty voice. Even though I don't know what he's saying, it almost seems like he's flirting with someone. Of course, that's a ridiculous idea.

He kind of purrs, "Mrph, mrph, mrph." Then there's a pause, and then a lot more "Mrphs." Another pause. "Mrph! Mrph?" Then I think he actually laughs. Out loud! I can't believe what I'm hearing. My serious, boring uncle is acting like an idiot in his own house! Adults can change, just like that! I should have expected it.

I'm only partly listening in on my uncle's conversation, of course. I'm also stewing about who might have called me and then hung up. That's making me so anxious that I jump up and start clearing the dishes off the table and stacking them in the dishwasher. I put the leftover macaroni and cheese into a covered dish and put that in the refrigerator. There's just enough for lunch tomorrow.

It's, maybe, three minutes after the mrphing stops that Uncle Martin comes back into the kitchen looking very rosy. I'm just finishing up. "That was Christine," he says. Now it's my turn to look blank. "Christine Stuart. The actor?"

I take a minute. Then I say, "Oh. Emily Carr," very indifferently, although that's not how I feel. I guess it bugs me that he's forgotten all about my phone call. Also that someone I thought might be my friend seems to be turning out to be his.

"She has a wonderful voice," Uncle Martin says. "And she's had a very interesting life." He sits back down at the table. "Didn't I smell brownies when I came in?

I point to the pan at the back of the stove. "Help yourself," I say. "I have school work to do."

I go into my bedroom – the one Uncle Martin moved out of so I wouldn't have to share with my little brother – and close the door. According to my mother, Uncle Martin has had a pretty bad time with the opposite sex. (This is in contrast to the fabulous string of experiences she's had herself.) He's met a couple of women he liked, but things never worked out. Maybe I should be hoping that he and Christine could get together, but the idea doesn't appeal to me. In fact, I think if there are any more changes in my life, I'll go off the deep end.

I'm sitting on the edge of the bed thinking black thoughts when Uncle Martin knocks on the door. "Nell?" he says.

"I'm doing my homework," I say. That's guaranteed to get him to leave me alone.

"Fine. I'm going downstairs to help Mike finish his Halloween costume."

"Nnnnn," I grunt, like I'm deeply involved in finding out what "n" equals.

"Thanks for supper," Uncle Martin says. After that it's quiet. I sit there another five minutes and then stretch out on the bed. I'm actually trying to decide which of my assignments I should work on, when I fall asleep. I seem to be doing that a lot lately.

*T*he next time I look at my watch, it's 8:30. I can hear Mikey splashing around in the bathtub, and a little later, fussing over where the Clifford toothpaste is. Then Uncle Martin knocks on the door. He can't find the tops to the red flannel pajamas Mom bought Mikey before she left, and Mikey won't go to bed in just the bottoms and his undershirt.

I get up and go out into the hall. I'm blinking like an owl at first, and I don't see how Uncle Martin can miss it, but he doesn't say anything. We both open drawers and look under the bed and search through the closet for what seems like at least ten minutes. Then Mikey remembers he took his pajama top to school in his backpack, in case he felt lonely.

Uncle Martin opens it up. There's an amazing amount of junk in there, including some things that we've been missing. Besides the happy face erasers, red, green, and gold glitter pens, crayons, alphabet stencils, smelly felts, various sizes and colours of paper, and many drawings, Mikey has stashed away an egg timer shaped like a bird, the raisins I couldn't find for oatmeal, some pencils Mom got me before she left with my name printed on them in gold, my red gym socks, another picture from the endless Mom, Mikey, and Merit series, and Uncle Martin's pocket lint roller.

"Why are you carrying all this junk around?" I ask him. Of course he has a perfectly inadequate answer.

"I need it."

"Why do you need it, Mike?" Uncle Martin asks.

"I need it so my pack won't feel empty," Mikey says. He's yawning and holding up his arms for someone to slide his pajama top down over them.

"But it's so heavy this way," Uncle Martin says.

Mikey shrugs. "I'm a man," he says. "I can take it."

Mikey is developing a thing about being a man. He hasn't spent much time around men, though, so I think he's a little confused about what that means, and ends up doing bizarre things like carrying heavy stuff in his backpack. Or trying to listen to jokes without laughing. Once I caught him taking swigs out of the vinegar bottle.

"What are you doing?" I asked him.

"It's a test for if I'm a man," he said. "I have to take three swallows without shivering."

Obviously, he feels he's passed. I wish there was some simple test I could take to tell me if I'm worth anything, but I don't think there is.

I only have one assignment due tomorrow. It's for L.A. We've just finished reading a novel called *Hatchet,* about a kid who has to survive alone out in the wilderness. Now I'm supposed to write a paragraph about the one thing I'd take with me if I had to go and live with a group of people on a desert island. I think I'd rather go off by myself, the way it happened in the novel, but that's not what we get to do, unfortunately.

When we discussed this in class, some people said they'd take ghetto blasters. Others said they'd take CDs. They thought they'd work together that way and be clever. Then Mr. Melnyk pointed out that we probably wouldn't have electricity.

Someone else said she'd take a blanket so she could sleep and stay warm. Then a guy asked if he could share it. Mr. Melnyk gave him the gears, but everyone heard what the guy said and laughed at it, so he got the attention he was looking for. Class discussions go that way a lot at JAWS.

I kept my mouth shut during this one, for a change. That way no one could laugh at me. But if you want to know what I really think, I think we'd need fire. My mother went to a wilderness camp out in the British Columbia interior, and she had to survive alone for three days. They let her take an axe and a knife and three matches. She didn't use any of the matches the first day, because she wanted to save them for emergencies. But on the second and third nights, she lit a fire. "It wasn't just for the heat," she told me. "It was also so I could have light at night. It made me feel like I was going to be okay."

That's why I say I'd take matches – so I could make a fire and keep it going all the time. If someone wanted to share it, that would be okay. But I'd keep a burning stick nearby. It isn't just wild animals that can be dangerous.

Chapter Eight

During the night – 4:00 a.m. according to my clock – I hear the phone ring again. Uncle Martin must pick it up down in the basement, where he's sleeping while we're here, because the answering machine doesn't come on. I think about getting up and checking to see who it is, but I guess I go back to sleep instead, because the next thing I remember is Uncle Martin knocking on the door. This time he comes right into my (formerly his) room.

"Nell," he says in a tired voice. He's wearing a worn-out terry cloth bathrobe that was once purple. Lots of the loops have pulled loose from the fabric and they stick out just asking to snag on something. I figure he must have had another call from JAWS and found out that I didn't go to school yesterday afternoon. What's wrong with those people? I ask inside my head. Don't they ever rest? Do they chain parent volunteers up at the front desk and force them to make attendance calls all night long?

The question I address to Uncle Martin is less dazzling. "Something the matter?" I ask, like I'm as innocent as noodles in soup.

"That was Alice," he says. "Your mother."

"I remember her name," I say.

"She had to call now because she won't be on the base by the time you get up. She's alarmed about an e-mail Mikey sent her yesterday. I explained what happened at Mary Chase and told her that everything's under control." He pauses. "She had a hard time understanding why Emily Carr was resurrected for the day, but I think I finally made her understand."

"I've had a little trouble with that myself," I say. I yawn and roll over onto my back.

"I was right to tell her that, wasn't I?" Uncle Martin waits for me to answer. When I don't, he asks, "Everything is under control, isn't it, Nell?"

"I guess so," I say. Depending, I don't add, on what you mean by everything.

"Despite my reassurances," he goes on, "your mother continues to be alarmed. And not just about Mike. She says you haven't answered any of her letters since she got there almost two months ago." He pauses again. I stay flat on my back and clam up. "Nell? Is that true?"

I yawn again, roll over on my side, and look in his direction. He doesn't have his ponytail any more and his hair is hanging forward. It makes him look kind of like an old-time movie star of the female persuasion – except for the jaw, of course. A woman with a jaw like that would probably be considering surgery. "I must have sent her a couple," I say. "I can't remember."

"She told me you'd say that."

"Or, maybe they got lost in cyberspace. I hear that happens all the time."

"She also told me you'd say that." Another pause. "Nell? Is something going on that I don't know about?"

That's such a complicated question that I hardly know where to begin, so I don't.

"Nell," Uncle Martin says, "Your mother assures me that something is wrong with you. She says she knows you very well and that by not writing, you're trying to make a point. Will you please tell me what it is?"

I don't half mind Uncle Martin's room. The walls are a kind of bluish-grey. There are no curtains – just wooden blinds that you can open and close. And he has a little TV mounted up in the corner over a bookcase that's the same kind of wood as the blinds. "Nell?" Uncle Martin says again.

The bedspread is pretty much the same colour as the walls. It's very tailored and I think that's a nice change from the kind of places girls usually sleep. "NELL?" Uncle Martin's starting to pink up and sound testy, so I decide I'd better say something.

"My point is," I say," that I'm upset with her." I roll over onto my back again. "She should have stayed here with us instead of running off to Bosnia. I don't think we should have to suffer for something that's happened on the other side of the world."

"Well," Uncle Martin says. He hems and haws like

people do when they don't know what else to say.

"But I don't see what's the big deal," I go on. "She already knows how I feel. I told her before she left. Why's she dragging you into it?"

"She says it's her mother's intuition." I don't respond. "For that matter," Uncle Martin says, "I don't think she's doing the right thing, either. But she's gone now. There's no use punishing her for something we can't do anything about."

"Right," I say.

"But she seems to think it's more than what you've mentioned. She thinks ... she feels, that is ... that you're in ... some kind of trouble." He pauses again. "Are you?"

"Am I in trouble with you?" I ask.

He shakes his head. "What about at school?"

"At school?" I ask. "Oh." Now I'm the one who pauses. "Not really. Nothing much. Except that I did stay home yesterday afternoon. I was worried about Mikey and I got home late for lunch because of his episode. So the school called about it."

"They didn't leave a message on the answering machine." He yawns and it's almost like he's talking to himself.

"Actually, they did, but ... I erased it. Accidentally." I'm almost telling the truth. I don't know if that makes up for the fact that I'm also almost lying.

"And that's all it is? Just this non-attendance from yesterday?"

"That's pretty much it," I say.

"Good," Uncle Martin says. He seems relieved, although I don't know if it's because I'm okay – he thinks – or because he isn't as clueless about kids as my mother made him think he was. Then he says, "I'm glad we had this little talk."

I knew some day he was going to say that to me! I think he's taken that line directly from some corny sixties TV show where the kids all have mothers and fathers and dogs that stay alive and do tricks. In fact, that's probably where all his parenting information comes from.

"I'll give you a note to take to school with you," he says, and then he goes back downstairs to bed. I think about calling him back – telling him what's really happening at school – but I don't. Instead I go back to sleep.

I don't wake up again until my alarm goes off. I call Mikey and make him some oatmeal while Uncle Martin shaves and gets ready for school. I put raisins in the oatmeal, since we've found them again, and I sprinkle brown sugar on the top. It looks so good I decide to have some myself.

Mikey starts spooning the oatmeal into his mouth like it's dessert. "I wish we had those buns Mom talked about with the chocolate pudding inside," he says.

"We don't," I say, but he doesn't give up easily.

"Mom makes toast animals sometimes." He smiles at me kind of hopefully.

"I've never been able to figure out how she does that, Mikey," I say. "The animals won't go into the toaster for me. But I can give you some sauerkraut for your oatmeal. I think this batch is about ready."

Even that doesn't get Mikey excited. He just smiles again and shows me that big space in the front where he's waiting for two shiny new teeth to come in.

Mikey's school day starts later than Uncle Martin's and mine, so Uncle Martin usually drops Mikey and me off at Mary Chase in the morning. Then Mikey goes into Jolly Gardens, which is what they call the before-and-after-school-care room, and I walk the few blocks to JAWS.

This morning, we're sitting in Uncle Martin's car waiting for him while he takes out the garbage and recycling. It's pickup day and he isn't about to miss it.

He comes back to the car looking pretty grim, but I don't ask him what's wrong, in case the answer is me.

When we get to Mary Chase, he tells Mikey to run into the school and asks me to wait for a minute. After my brother's out of earshot, Uncle Martin says, "Someone smashed all the pumpkins you put up on the fence. I didn't want to say it in front of Mike because then we'd never get him to go to school."

"Oh?" I say, like I've got nothing but the weather on my mind.

If you were in my situation, would you wonder if the

smashed pumpkins and the anonymous phone call last night had something to do with each other? Maybe not. But the thing is – and I know this makes me sound paranoid – I do.

"What a rotten prank," Uncle Martin goes on. "He'll notice they aren't there tonight."

"For sure."

"Well, I have to get to school now," he says. "Let's try to think of something." I open the door and start to get out of the car. "Oh ... and Nell?" I turn back toward him. "Have a nice day." Then he drives off. He's just made a little joke, if he only knew it. It may be his first since we moved in.

Chapter Nine

Mikey is flying high after we come home at noon. The Clifford costume he and Uncle Martin have made isn't anything exceptional. It looks like it's made out of another of Uncle Martin's old bathrobes – reddish-brown this time instead of purple. And for the mask, they've stitched soft, floppy ears onto a balaclava. Still, I have to admit that Mikey seems quite doggy and cheerful when he's dressed up.

He doesn't really look that big, of course. I guess there are limits to Uncle Martin's creative genius. But Mikey obviously believes he's bigger than everybody else now, so that's how he feels. All the way back to school he keeps barking at people and saying, "I'm Clifford the Big Red Dog." Then he pulls off his mask and flashes the gap in his front teeth. "How do you like me?" he asks.

Everyone seems to like him fine. They smile and wave and say friendly things to him. One really little girl is dressed up like an angel with white pantyhose wings and a tinsel halo that hangs down over one eye. She asks him, "Are you really a dog?" (She does this after he's taken his mask off.)

Mikey says, "Woof! Woof!" which seems to convince her.

As I'm leaving Mary Chase and heading off for JAWS, some little kid asks me who I'm supposed to be. "Supergirl," I tell him. "I just haven't gone into a phone booth and changed my clothes yet." Honestly, I wish I really could do that. I'd pull on my cape and my long tights and leap over tall buildings. Maybe right a few wrongs. Or haul my mother back from Bosnia so fast the two chevron stripes and the maple leaf she wears on her arm would fly off and get a life of their own. Instead, I'm stuck in Mr. Melnyk's classroom until 3:15 with a few other people who aren't going to the dance.

Two kids I've never seen before are playing chess over by his desk, and another boy and girl actually seem to be working on assignments. The boy keeps coming up to Mr. Melnyk's desk, though, handing him work and asking, "Now can I go to the dance?"

So far, Mr. Melnyk has looked it over, said stuff like, "No, Blaine, you've forgotten question four," and sent him back to his seat. I guess this Blaine really wants to go to the gym and stand around in the dark, smelling old sweat socks that have fallen down into the bleachers, and watching a few couples hold each other up in the middle of the floor. I'm not kidding when I say that the music at these events is so loud you can get nerve damage if you listen to it for more than fifteen minutes. And I know what I'm talking about. We had dances at Mason Middle School last year and even there they were awful.

*T*here is one familiar person in the room. (Besides Mr. Melnyk, I mean.) Sam Hashi is sitting at the other computer, right next to me. He's from my Foods class, remember? He's not a long-lost friend or anything, but he's never been nasty, or joined in with Shane, so I don't mind him being here.

I don't say anything when I first sit down. Sam looks really involved in making some kind of personalized screen saver, so I try to look like I have something specific in mind to do. After I surf the main menu for a while, I decide to check out the recipes on a vegetarian Web site I sometimes visit. I'm always thinking about eliminating meat from my diet. Up to now I haven't put much effort into doing it, but Uncle Martin's cooking is suddenly making the idea very attractive. There'd be so much of it I could turn down for ethical reasons.

After about ten minutes or so, Sam kind of checks me out from the corners of his eyes and asks, "How come you're in here?"

"I'm not into dancing," I say. "How come you're in here?"

"I'd rather work on the computer."

"Oh."

"I don't have one at home," he goes on, like he has to explain. He makes an adjustment on his computer screen and turns the background from purple to crimson. Then he surprises me by speaking again. "Do you know who Bonnie Lewis is?" I give him a blank look. "She's pretty tall and has red and black streaks in her hair," he says. "It's kind of rough looking." He pauses. "Oh, and she has rings in her lower lip."

"No," I say, "I don't know her." But into my mind comes this picture of the girl with Shane at the Highlands Centre yesterday.

"You sure?" Sam's made the background of his computer screen completely black, with red firecracker lights bursting all over it. That last part is happening in my stomach too.

"Is there some reason I should know her?" I ask faintly.

"Bonnie and two of her friends were looking for you yesterday, before last period."

"Me?" I squeak. "Why were they looking for me?"

"She wanted to know where you live. I imagine it's because she's Shane's girlfriend." Now the fireworks turn white. And so do I.

"It figures," I sigh. I've got a recipe for Moroccan Carrots with Orange Glaze on my screen, with a colour illustration. It makes me think of the smashed pumpkins in Uncle Martin's back alley, though, so I get rid of it. I'm not sure I'll ever care for orange again.

Sam actually turns away from his computer keyboard and looks directly at me. "Are you all right?" he asks. Fireworks keep on bursting. One, two, three. One, two, three.

"Sure," I say, but my mouth feels very dry all of a sudden. "Why was she asking you?"

"Do you know my brother Ziad?"

"I don't know anybody at this school," I blurt. "You're one of the few kids who even speaks to me."

"Well," Sam says. "You're new." I nod. "And you're smart." I make a face. "Or you sound like it." That could be a dig, but the way he says it, it doesn't feel that way.

He goes back to his computer, plays around a bit, and comes up with red-and-white stripes that wrap the screen. "People call my brother Zee," he says, "partly because his name is unusual. But mostly because he's big and ... well, he's ... he likes to rescue people." Sam makes a zigzag through the air with his hand. I finally get it then. Zorro. He makes the sign of the Zee. I've grown up saying zed like most Canadians, or I would have made the connection sooner.

"My father says Ziad minds everybody's business but his own," Sam says. The white stripes get thinner and thinner until the whole screen is solid red. "It's not that he isn't a good person. But he isn't very interested in school and sometimes – he makes my parents unhappy."

"Who doesn't?" I ask.

"I try not to," Sam says. I'm pretty sure he's telling the truth about that.

I wait a while for Sam to connect the dot that has Bonnie on it with the one that's labeled Zee or Ziad or whatever. When it looks like he isn't going to, I click open the solitaire game that's on the network. I'm hoping it will calm me down.

I've been playing it for a while when Sam finally says, "Ziad knows everything that's going on in the school. Especially everything that's going on in Grade Nine." When I still don't seem to clue in to the connection, he adds, "Bonnie and Ziad are both in Grade Nine. They're also in the same homeroom."

"They're friends?" I ask.

"They know each other. And Bonnie probably figures if you and I are both in Grade Seven, then I must know you. It's not that big a school."

"You didn't tell her where I live, did you?"

"How could I? I don't know."

Just about then, Mr. Melnyk walks over and stands behind me. "Are you a solitaire player, Nell?" he asks.

I think the answer to that should be obvious, but I mumble, "Sometimes. It gives me something to do."

I figure next he'll say something lame like, "Oh, I guess we aren't giving you enough homework to keep you busy, chuckle, chuckle," but instead he asks me to come over to his desk. There's a chair beside it and he motions for me to sit down.

"I just want to tell you," he says in this very whispery voice, "that I'm quite unhappy about what happened in Foods yesterday." He obviously doesn't mean the extra baking powder in our muffins.

"There haven't been any repercussions, have there?"

"No," I say. "At least ... no."

"Is there something I should know?" he asks. I shake my head.

Mr. Melnyk is beginning to act like the adults in my family. He's serious all the time. He throws big words around. And he expects me to tell him the things he really should know on his own.

"Well," he says, "please let me know if there are any more problems. We have zero tolerance for that kind of thing in this school." (That seems to be everybody's favourite expression.) Then he pushes back from his desk, stands up, and in the big teacher voice says, "I'm going to check on things in the gym. I'll be back in about a five minutes."

"Was that about what happened in Foods yesterday?" Sam asks when I'm at my computer again.

"I guess," I say. I just sit there and watch my hands twisting in my lap.

"Did you mention about Bonnie?"

"No. Where would that get me?"

"What are you going to do then?" Sam asks.

I shrug. "What difference does it make, anyway?"

My solitaire game isn't going anywhere, so I decide to access Uncle Martin's e-mail account. I'm wondering if there might be something from my mother. There is. She must have sent it within the last few hours, because she's talking about the Halloween party they put on for the kids in V.K. It sounds like they're having a lot more fun across the ocean than I am.

Subject:	**Happy Halloween!**
Date:	October 31, 2000 21:10:29
From:	"MCpl.AS.Mackelwain,ASU Edmonton, 582-5418,0900" <mail466@dnd.ca>
To:	mmackelwain@hotmail.com

Hi, Kids!

I'm sorry I had to call so early this morning and didn't get to talk to either of you. But all the later slots were signed up, so I took what I could get. I was a little worried about ghosts at Mary Chase, but Martin explained – as much as Martin ever explains, that is. I'm trusting you're both all right.

I heard about your Clifford costume, Lester B., and it sounds great. Nell, he says you're not going to the dance and aren't dressing up. Even so, I hope you're having some fun during the day. I just wish I could hear what you're doing in your own words. Write me, please.

Today two of us went by the village school with Halloween treats for the kids. This wasn't a day off for us, but we got permission to go as part of our stabilization effort. We couldn't dress up because we were on official business, of course, so we wore our combat uniforms. At home that would look like a costume, but here it's what we wear every day.

We didn't want to take candy because we're supposed to be teaching these kids about good nutrition, so we brought juice boxes and fruit instead. They liked the food and were very excited to see us.

We've learned that the name of the little boy with the orange jacket is Edin Hidic. He's five but isn't in school for some reason, because he was waiting for us outside when we got there. Lorna wasn't with us and he still won't come to anyone else, so he just stood by the door and watched.

The teacher, Mr. Asanagic, tells us Edin's brother, Mirsad, is in school and will share some of the treats we left with him. He and Edin's parents were both killed during the war and their fifteen-year-old sister is looking after them. We're going to find out where they live and take some water and food to them if we can.

We tried to tell the students about our Halloween customs in Canada. Elvis was with us and he translated. We had a difficult time making them understand about pumpkins, though. They don't seem to grow them locally. It would have been wonderful to show the students pictures of the pumpkins you have out on Martin's back fence.

We wanted to read a Halloween story, but the language problem made it difficult. If we'd had picture books, it wouldn't have mattered so much. I'm wondering, Lester B., if you'd like to share some of yours? Just while I'm here, of course. Maybe these children would like to read about Clifford.

The kids at the school had finished all the fruit and juice when we left, so we gave each child a quarter of a chocolate bar – just enough to make it a really special day. We wanted to give out Canadian chocolate, but most of our supplies come from Germany, so it was German chocolate we gave them. We all think it's excellent.

There's a beautiful harvest moon tonight. It really does appear to have a face. Whether a man's or a woman's, I can't say, but I wish I could see yours as clearly.
Love you and miss you,

Mom

PS I managed to get a good phone-out slot on Saturday, so you should be hearing from me about 16:00 then. (That's four p.m. to you.) I can't wait to talk to you. "MCpl.AS.Mackelwain,ASU Edmonton,582-5418,0900" e-mail:466@dnd.ca

Since my mom complains again that I haven't written, I decide to do it, just so she'll quit harping on the subject. I don't tell her the story of the three little pumpkins and how I think they got smashed, though. Actually, I don't tell her much at all, but she'll get the point.

Subject:	**I'm Fine**
Date:	October 31, 2000
From:	<mmackelwain@hotmail.com>
To:	mail466@dnd.ca

Dear Mother,
I am fine. How are you?
Love,
Nell

Just as I'm sending that elaborate message off to my mother, Mr. Melnyk comes back into the room. At least, I hear footsteps and sense that someone is standing behind me, so I THINK it's Mr. Melnyk. I really don't want to talk, and I try to act very engrossed so he'll go away. He doesn't. I'm thinking it's pretty rude to read personal stuff over someone's shoulder, so I click off the e-mail and turn around. Then my heart falls into my stomach and my stomach ends up down around my ankles.

It isn't Mr. Melnyk standing behind me. It's a tall girl with two rings in her bottom lip, and hair that's streaked red and black and looks like it's been cut with a lawn mower. It's also the girl who freaked me out yesterday when I was hiding in the bushes. Sam's description fits her perfectly, so I guess her name must be Bonnie, although it's kind of an old-fashioned name for someone who looks as tough as she does.

"Hiding out with Sam?" she asks. She gives me a mean smile.

"I'm not hiding," I say. I straighten up and hope my insides will go back into place. "I'm working."

She looks at my computer screen, which by now is empty and green. She smirks, and steps closer. "You're an ugly little mouse, and you're hiding out because you're scared."

I look around, but no one else in the room is paying any attention to us. The girl doing homework has her nose down on her paper. The chess kids are now wearing headphones and hooked up to a video. Blaine has apparently gone to the dance. And Sam is doing the usual. This time, though, his screen is blue with doves flying around on it. It's a nice touch, but Bonnie doesn't seem to notice.

"I am not hiding," I say.

Bonnie puts one hand on the back of my chair, the other on the computer table, and leans down toward me. I notice she has words scratched into the fingers of the hand on the table. "L-O-V-E," the scabby letters say. I'm pretty sure she wasn't thinking of me when she put them there.

"I have a message for you, Mouse," she says. She's smiling again. "Or, excuse me. You like to be called Smelly, don't you?" Now the smile disappears and she leans in even closer. "Shane belongs to me. If you ever touch him again or get him in trouble, I'll make you pay."

This would be the place to tell her that I have rights and don't need to tolerate her put-downs, or his. It would also be a very good place to point out that he isn't much of a boyfriend if she has to defend him from his own actions. I wouldn't have to lose my temper or anything. I could speak calmly and rationally. But I'm scared and angry – you know my pattern by now – so what I say is, "Why would I want to touch him? He makes me sick."

She throws a few choice words at me. Then I hear Sam say, "She wasn't trying to make trouble, Bonnie. Shane bugs her a lot and she was just trying to get him to leave her alone."

"Stay out of this, Sam," Bonnie snaps. "It's none of your

business." She gives me a little push. I almost lose my balance, but I straighten back up again. "Did you hear me, Smelly? We know where you live, and we'll smash more than pumpkins if we come by your house again."

That's when Mr. Melnyk comes back. He crosses the room in two steps, and demands, "What are you doing in here, Bonnie? You know you're not supposed to leave the dance area."

"I forgot," she says. She flashes him this cheesy smile. "I'm just visiting. I'll go back to the dance now."

"I'm afraid you can't do that," Mr. Melnyk says. "You know the rule. If you leave the dance area, you aren't allowed back in."

That takes care of Bonnie for a while. She makes a stink, but in the end, I guess Mr. Melnyk escorts her to her locker and then probably right out the front door of the school.

I take a computer manual and throw it on the floor when they're gone. "I hate this place!" I say. "I wish I'd never come here! And I wouldn't have, if my mother hadn't made me!" That's when I notice I have everyone's attention. The two video guys are watching with their mouths open. They've even taken off their headphones so they can hear better. And the homework girl has stopped writing. She's gaping at me and holding her pencil in mid-air.

"Could you give me some privacy?" I snap. The girl does, but the boys keep on staring. I glare at them.

"Nell," Sam says. His dark brown eyes look sympathetic, even though now I'm glaring at him. Finally, I turn back toward my computer, and I think the boys re-hook themselves to the TV, although I'm not watching them any-more, so I can't say for sure.

After a bit, Sam says, "Maybe you should report this."

I dig a Kleenex out of my pocket and blow my nose. "Reporting what Shane did is what got me into this mess in the first place. Why should this be any different? Especially now that his girlfriend knows where I live!"

"You mean Bonnie came to your house?" Sam asks.

"You heard what she said! Someone came and smashed all our pumpkins last night! Oh, and I also got an anony-mous phone call."

"From her?"

"Duh!" I say. "Anonymous means I don't know who it was, but I'll bet it was either her or her boyfriend." I'm so rude I'm surprised Sam doesn't walk out on me.

He frowns. "Shane is mostly talk," he says. "Bonnie's the one to worry about."

I bang my hands down on the table. "What's her problem?" I say. It's possible I sound whiney.

Sam shrugs. "I only know what Ziad says."

"And?"

"Ziad says that after her parents' divorce, Bonnie used to live with her dad. He let her do whatever she wanted. Then last year he got married again, and now his wife is trying to make Bonnie toe the line."

"But that's what parents are supposed to do."

Sam nods. "Bonnie told Ziad that she hates her stepmother and she's mad at her father for getting married, so she's doing everything she can to get them to kick her out. She thinks it would be cool to live in a foster home."

"That's sick!" I say.

"I agree. Family matters more than anything."

I'm getting good at sighing by now, and I make this one long and deep. Then I ask, "Any ideas about what I do now?"

"I think you should call your father and see if he can pick you up – in case Bonnie's waiting for you outside the school."

"I don't have a father on active duty," I tell Sam, and swallow a couple of times.

"Call your mother, then. She can drive, can't she?"

"Oh, sure. She drives all over the place, but she won't come to get me."

"Is she at work?"

"No," I blurt. "She's at war! Or trying to stop one! Don't ask me to make sense out of my mother's life!" Sam looks at me like I'm crazy. "She's in Bosnia," I say. "My mother's a peacekeeper."

He whistles softly through his teeth. "Bosnia!" he says. "Isn't that where they dug up all those bodies?"

"That was a few years ago. What they're digging up now is land mines."

"Weren't most of the people who were killed Muslims?"

"I guess so," I say. "What does it matter who they were?"

Sam is quiet for a bit. Then he says, "Me and my family

are Muslim, so it matters to me."

"I'm sorry," I say, and really mean it. Sometimes I wish I could take back the things that come out of my mouth.

Sam just looks at me for a moment. Then he whistles again. "You mean your mother wears an army uniform and carries a gun?"

"Most of the time. She also drives trucks and jeeps."

He shakes his head like he just can't get over what I've told him. "My mother stays at home. She doesn't even know how to drive. Dad has a taxi, and if she needs to go somewhere, he takes her."

By now it's 3:10, and Mr. Melnyk isn't back yet. I start to gather my things up and put them in my school bag. "My little brother goes to Mary Chase School," I explain. "I have to pick him up on time today. Otherwise, he'll be so hyped-up on sugar that he may just take off on his own and get lost." Then I sit down again and look over at Sam. "Do you have any more advice?"

He does. "I can't walk with you," he says, "because I have to catch the bus here and I'll get into trouble if I'm late coming home from school. But if we both go out the side door, I can watch you run along the edge of the soccer field. I'll be able to see you until you get to the lights at 111th Avenue. If there's trouble, I'll run back to the office, even if it means missing the bus. You'll be on your own after that, but once you cross 111th, I think you'll be okay."

Bonnie's already been to my house, so I don't think the fact that 111th is a very busy street will keep her away. But

I don't have any other ideas, better or worse, so that's what I end up doing. At exactly 3:15, I leave the school. "Go as fast as you can," Sam says at the door.

"I will," I say. I can run like the wind if I have to. And that's exactly what I do.

Chapter Ten

*T*hat's pretty much it for my Halloween. When I get to Mary Chase, I'm still in one piece and not totally terrified anymore. I help Mikey gather up all his loot, herd him out the school door and back to Uncle Martin's house without any trouble. (I'm not counting the two cats he runs up trees on the way home when I say that. Or the fact that he pretends to do the dog thing to a fire hydrant across the street from school.)

Mikey goes right in to the study and finds the new letter from Mom, so he's ecstatic about that. While he's reading, Uncle Martin comes home, slips around to the back of the house, and puts three very fancy jack-o'-lanterns up on the fence posts.

"Do you think he'll notice the difference?" he asks. "I brought them from my art room."

"Hard to tell," I say, trying to look like I'm in pain.

I've decided it would be a good idea for me to pretty much disappear from the world for the next twenty-four hours at least, so I tell Uncle Martin I have a stomach ache and need to lie down. He acts concerned but doesn't ask a lot of questions like my mother would – where it hurts, when it started, things like that.

I keep on about my stomach ache after dinner, so Uncle Martin takes Mikey out trick-or-treating and leaves me at home, lying on the couch in the living room with a hot water bottle on my stomach. He tells me I'll still have to answer the door, which in some ways is as scary as going outside.

At first I try peeking out at callers through the little fish-eye thing in the door before I open it, but that doesn't help. They all seem far away and look like miniature cone-heads. If I pull back the corner of the living-room curtain a bit, though, I can see the doorway pretty clearly. That's what I end up doing every time I hear someone yell, "Trick or Treat!" or "Halloween Apples!" A couple of times I look out and think I see someone standing in the shadow of the spruce tree beside the driveway, but I guess it's my imagination. All our callers turn out to be normal kids.

Uncle Martin bought Malted Milk Balls in little cellophane packages to give out as treats. I'm just getting up to get myself a couple, when I hear him and Mikey coming up the back steps. I jump back on the couch, grab the hot water bottle, and plunk it on my stomach. The water in it is still gurgling when they come into the living room.

"Did you see the pumpkins?" Mikey asks. "They look even fancier than when we carved them. Isn't that great?" He's carrying a pillowcase half-filled with candy and he puts it on the floor. Then he sits down on the couch, pulls off his mask, and lets out a long bow-wow. I think that can be translated as, "I'm home and I've really cleaned up tonight!"

*T*he next morning I tell Uncle Martin that I'm still feeling ill and don't want to go to school. That doesn't go over really well with him because he's a firm believer in regular school attendance, so I have to moan and lay it on a little thick. Then Mikey moans even louder about how he can't go to school without me, how he hates staying at Jolly Gardens for lunch, how he isn't feeling well himself. But I don't give in like I usually do. In the end, Uncle Martin makes Mikey a lunch and takes him off to Mary Chase.

I don't have a great day by myself. I stay inside and keep the curtains closed. I watch chickadees and nuthatches come to the feeder just outside the French doors in the dining room. I sleep. I read a little bit. I try to watch TV, but there's nothing on. I even do a bit of homework. But all day long I feel like I'm under house arrest and being watched.

By the time Mikey and Uncle Martin come back home again, I'm in my room with the door shut, pretending to be asleep. Mikey's very excited about something. I can hear Uncle Martin shushing him, but he eventually bursts into the room to tell me that all the kids in his class are going to collect books for the school in Bosnia our mother wrote about.

Apparently he showed Mrs. Montcrieff Mom's latest e-mail and she got all excited about it. Now Mikey wants to go through his pack and send them all his school supplies, including MY pencils with MY name on them. We argue about that for a bit, but finally I tell him to go ahead.

Mikey also wants to take up a collection for Edin and his brother. He wants to know why Edin isn't in school if he's five. He wonders how his sister can be the head of the family when she's only fifteen. "Would you be able to do that, Nell?" he asks me.

"Of course, Mikey," I tell him. "I practically am already."

After Mikey's in bed and Uncle Martin is working on whatever he works on when he's down in the basement, I decide to call Sam. I'm hoping he can tell me what happened at school today and whether it's safe for me to come back. I look in the phone book. There's only one Hashi listed, and the address looks reasonable, but when I punch in the number, a woman answers.

"May I please speak to Sam?" I ask.

She says, "Is wrong number."

"Excuse me?" I say.

"No Sam here," she says again and hangs up.

I decide to put the phone on the charger. Uncle Martin keeps it on the lowest shelf of a little bookcase beside the front window. I'm just straightening up from doing that, when I notice a lump of something underneath the mail slot in the front door. I take a closer look. Then I scream.

Uncle Martin comes pounding up the stairs when he hears me. "What is it, Nell?" he shouts. He looks where I'm pointing and then looks back at me. "Is that all?" he says. "I thought something serious had happened."

By now Mikey is down on his hands and knees taking a close look. "Careful, Mike," Uncle Martin says. "It was probably sick and crawled out of its hole to die. There'll be germs." He picks up the dead mouse by the tail and carries it out to the trash. Afterwards he washes his hands. I wish I could deal with the whole thing that easily.

*U*ncle Martin figures I don't seem sick enough to miss two days of school, and I can't produce spots or welts or swollen glands just because I want to, so on Thursday I have to go back to school. I try to be philosophical about it, but the closer I get to JAWS, the more I feel like throwing up. I decide to come in the side door, the way I left on Halloween, and take the back stairs to my locker. It's only about five minutes until the first bell rings, but there still aren't many people in this part of the building.

As I walk down the hallway, though, I see Sam standing by my locker. I guess he's been waiting for me, which is quite a surprise. It's the first time a kid at JAWS has ever gone out of the way to talk to me.

"You didn't come to school yesterday," he says.

"No," I say. I have to look up to him when I say it, because if I don't, he ends up talking to the top of my head.

"I knew nothing had happened to you, though. Ziad would have told me."

"Nothing happened. I ... wasn't feeling well."

Sam nods like he believes that – or doesn't, and is just going along with me. I can't tell which. Then he says, "Bonnie's been suspended for three days."

"Because of me?" I ask. "How did they find out?"

"They didn't. But after Mr. Melnyk put her out the front door, Bonnie went around to the gym. Someone had opened the door a crack and she got back in. None of the teachers on supervision knew she wasn't supposed to be in there, so she stayed to the end of the dance. When Mr. Melnyk saw her leaving, he went after her, and she took off."

Sam watches me standing there for a minute. "It's almost time for class," he says. "Don't you need to take off your coat and put your stuff away?"

"I'm trying to decide if I'm staying," I say, although what I'm really trying to decide is whether or not I want to open my locker while he's standing there.

People at JAWS are all carried away with decorating theirs. Girls tape up pictures of their favorite movie and rock stars. Some of them have made regular little shrines to their families or their cats and dogs. Guys plaster the inside of their locker doors with posters of girls and professional athletes, although if the girlie pictures are at all pornographic, Mr. Wills, the principal, takes them down during locker inspection. He's very big on that kind of thing.

I don't have anything on the inside of my locker door except my class schedule. There are four days in the JAWS week, instead of five – I guess in case school life isn't confusing enough already. I'm not exactly stupid, but after almost two months, I still have to check my schedule every day to make sure which classes I have and when I have them.

Anyway, I figure Sam will think the inside of my locker is pretty boring, so I try to keep the door between us. He peeks around anyway.

"You're very tidy," he says. "That's good."

I'm not used to getting compliments from people my age, so I kind of gape at him. Then I close my locker door and fasten the lock.

Now Sam examines that. "This is a school lock," he says.

"Yes," I say.

"You should buy one of your own," he tells me. "Homeroom teachers keep the combinations written down for all school locks. It's easy for someone to look over the teacher's shoulder and get your combination, or your address. Even your phone number."

I guess that explains a few things. "How do you know all this stuff?" I ask.

"Ziad," Sam says.

"He's the one who told you that Bonnie's suspended?"

"As soon as she comes back. She wasn't here yesterday either."

"I guess I wasted a perfectly good non-sick day then," I say, but I get the feeling that Sam's never had one of those in his life and doesn't know what I'm talking about.

"Ziad's watching us now," he says, "just so he'll know what you look like and can recognize you if you're in trouble. You don't mind, do you?"

I look around but don't see anyone. "Don't tell me," I say. "He's wearing a mask and a black cape, but I can't see him because he's basically invisible to anyone except you."

One good thing about Sam is he doesn't let the things I blurt out bother him. He gestures toward the elevator in the north corner of the hall with the hand that's holding his bookbag. It's really scuffed up, I notice, and one of the handles is completely covered with silver duct tape.

"I thought the elevator was only for the boy in Grade Nine who's in a wheelchair," I say. "Anyway, why doesn't Ziad just come over and introduce himself?"

Sam shrugs. "Ziad has his own way of doing things." He turns to go to class, then stops and turns back again. "Did you call me last night?"

"Yes," I say. "But a woman answered and said there was no one named Sam there."

"That was my mother. Sam isn't the name my parents call me by."

"What name do they use?" I ask him, but he doesn't answer.

"I won't be able to talk to you on the phone."

"Is it because of your religion?" When Sam doesn't answer

that question either, I say, "Because your parents don't have to be offended by mine. I don't exactly have one."

"They wouldn't understand that," he says. "But the reason I can't talk to you on the phone is because you're a girl. It isn't good for a girl to call a boy. And it would be even worse if I called you. It would mean that I think you're ... you know ... wild. Your family would be right to be insulted."

Just then the bell rings. Sam says goodbye, turns and walks down the hall to class. And I figure, wild girl or not, that I might as well go to mine.

I wish Sam wanted to talk about his name. It couldn't be any weirder than my brother's and mine. Where it says "Nellie Letitia Hopkins" on my birth certificate? That's after Nellie Letitia McClung. You already know the name Mikey got stuck with.

Mom thinks being named after great people can make you great yourself. But what difference does it make if Lester B. Pearson helped settle a war somewhere? Or if Nellie McClung went around lecturing for women's rights?

Mikey's a lot more likely to be a dog groomer or street performer than prime minister. And as for me getting up in front of people for any reason, forget it. I mostly speak out when I'm mad, and as you've already seen, it's usually a disaster when I do. I intend to keep my mouth CLOSED for the rest of my life.

Chapter Eleven

*T*hursday was endless, for no particular reason, and now it's Friday. I'm grateful it's the end of the week and all that, but Friday means we start Day One of our timetable again. And that means I have to go to Foods and deal with Shane. It also means I'll be able to talk to Sam and get filled in on what Ziad knows, which is good, but not good enough to make me want to come to school.

Anyway, before I get to Foods I have to go to L.A. and participate in this desert island thing. We're now into a procedure where we need to find two other people who agree with our choice. So far I've only been able to find one. Her name is Karen Lavoie and she wasn't very hard to convince. I said, "I think if we don't take matches we'll be cold and hungry and lonely." And she said, "Okay."

Today's my last day to find a second person, though, and I'm not overly optimistic. For one thing, I'm tired, and it takes way more energy to be convincing than to be convinced. For another, I don't have as much faith in my own opinions as I used to.

By the time I get to Foods, I'm even more tired. People yawned at me when I tried to sell them on my matches, then I yawned through Math, which is not my finest subject. Now I'm listening to Mr. Melnyk again. This time he's talking about our next Foods unit, which will be "Foods for Survival." We're going to learn to make high-energy food logs out of peanut butter, dried fruit, and seeds, some kind of drink that keeps us from dehydrating, and other equally exciting stuff. We may even make pemmican and dried apples. Then in January we're going on a winter survival sleepover at a wilderness centre down in the river valley by the Muttart Conservatory.

This is all a yawner too, as far as I'm concerned. I thought survival was when your plane went down in the bush and you had to live on berries, like that kid did in *Hatchet.* Or like my mother did out in British Columbia. Preparing for at least a month and a half in order to survive sounds like a planned holiday to me. I'm saving another non-sick day especially for the sleepover.

*W*hen Mr. Melnyk finishes talking, he expects us to copy pages and pages of notes and recipes. Priscilla gets right to work with her pen and magnifying glass. Sam doesn't look enthusiastic, but he starts writing. Shane draws the usual in his notebook, then sits with his arms crossed and stares daggers at me. If he could catch my eye, I'm sure he'd do his little clawing-the-air thing.

I tell Mr. Melnyk I can't see very well and ask him if I

can move closer to the screen. "Okay," he says, but he gives me an inquiring look as I move my chair as far away from Shane as I can get. I do my best to concentrate on my copying. It's quiet in the room, and now that I'm away from Shane, it isn't absolutely impossible.

Just as the bell rings and I'm gathering up my stuff for lunch, Sam walks by and drops a note in my bookbag. Right after that, Shane walks by and also drops a note in my bookbag. Then Mr. Melnyk comes over to me and says, "Could you wait a minute after class, Nell?" Suddenly I'm in great demand.

When we're back by his desk, Mr. Melnyk tells me that he and Mr. Wills would like to talk to me during the noon hour.

"I can't," I say. "I have to pick up my little brother and take him home for lunch."

"It's important," Mr. Melnyk says. "Is there any way your mother could do it just for today?"

I guess he hasn't read my registration forms either. "I live with my uncle," I say, "and he's at work. My mother is out of the country."

"Oh," Mr. Melnyk says. "Well then, let's meet after school."

"I have the same problem then," I tell him. I'm walking toward the door as I speak. "I have to get going now. My little brother will get anxious if I'm late." Then I beat it out of the room.

Mikey and I have a variation of my famous tomato soup lunch. The variation is that I put half a can of soup in each of our bowls, add milk and heat it in the microwave. I'm not into cooking very much right now. I tell Mikey if he doesn't complain I'll let him have three treats after lunch instead of the one he's supposed to have. He becomes very cooperative.

I take the notes out and read them while I'm eating. Sam's just says, "Meet me at your locker when you get back from lunch." The one from Shane isn't what I was expecting. I thought there'd be the usual drawing of a claw and something like, "You're dead meat, Smelly." Instead, there's a drawing of two eyes. They're outlined so they look Egyptian and exotic. Underneath them someone has written – definitely not Shane because I've seen his writing on class notes – "I'm watching you." I guess that's to let me know that even if Bonnie isn't in school, she has friends to help her out.

I tell myself that if I got rested up and felt a little less anxious, I'd be able to see right through the stuff Shane and Bonnie are doing. They mostly have power over me because I'm letting them. I'm not rested up, though. In fact, I'm so jittery that words are coming into my head. I try to keep them out, but they come anyway. "I miss my mother," is what they say. "I miss my mother. I wish she was here."

Just as we're finishing lunch, the phone rings. I figure it's Bonnie and want to let it ring, but Mikey makes a beeline for it. It turns out to be the secretary from JAWS. She tells him Mr. Wills would like me to report to his office as soon as I get back to school.

After Mikey passes on the message, he remembers he has a book that's overdue at the school library. It takes us so long to find it that the bell is ringing as I come in the side door. That's my routine approach to the school now. I go directly into the office. Sam wouldn't be at my locker any more, anyhow.

The secretary at JAWS isn't friendly like the one at Mikey's school. Maybe she hasn't figured out yet that kids are the reason the school is here. She's usually at the computer clicking away whenever I see her, although I don't know how she manages, because she's got artificial fingernails that are as long as the claws Shane insists on drawing on all his Foods assignments. They're painted a fruity, bluish-red colour, and she has a ring on almost every finger.

I wait quite a while at the counter. Then I clear my throat and say, "Excuse me."

She looks up, although not right away. "Can I help you?" she asks, like she's just amazed to see a student standing in the office.

"I'm Nell Hopkins," I say. "I'm supposed to see Mr. Wills."

"No," she says. She frowns while she looks through a bunch of pink stickies placed around her computer screen.

"Someone called me at lunch and left a message with my brother."

"Oh, NELLIE Hopkins." She flashes a smile that's about as phony as Bonnie's, and shows me her perfect white teeth. "I'll see if Mr. Wills can talk to you."

She knocks on the door to Mr. Wills's office, opens it, and goes in. When she comes back out, she says, "He's busy at the moment," and is even less friendly than she was earlier, if that's possible. "Go to class and he'll call for you when he's ready."

I don't know what happened in Mr. Wills's office that tightened her crank, but I suddenly feel like I've had enough. Now I'll need to get a late slip and drag into class with everybody staring at me, when I wasn't late in the first place. I may have to sit on pins and needles all afternoon waiting for Mr. Wills to be ready to talk to me. And if I do get called out of class, I'll have to make up everything I miss plus do all the homework I normally have.

"I'm not feeling well," I say, walking out the door. "I'm going home." I think the secretary calls something after me about school policy and signing out, but I don't care. I'm fed up. I QUIT!

I walk toward the front door and am just about to open it when I remember that route out of the school isn't one hundred percent safe. I make a U-turn and go back the way I came. I have to. I can't get to the side door otherwise, and that's the only way in and out of the school I trust anymore.

I sail past the office again and I'm pretty far down the hall when I hear someone yell, "STOP!" I mean really yell it. People can probably hear it up in the classrooms on the second floor. I do what the voice says and turn around. Mr. Wills is standing in front of the office. He motions me to come back. I walk toward him, but I make myself a promise that if he calls me Nellie, I'll turn and run for the exit and I'll never come back to JAWS, no matter what my mother and Uncle Martin have to say about it.

*M*r. Wills isn't what you'd call "cool." His skin is kind of grey and he's a little on the paunchy side. Also, his hair is pretty much gone. That's normal for a principal, of course, and I suppose he can't help it. But he wears these aviator glasses that you mostly see on retired teachers who sit around drinking coffee and smoking in the malls. And he has stainless steel caps on two of his front teeth. Why he can't go to a regular dentist is beyond me.

"Miss Hopkins?" he says when I get as close as I'm going to. He has my attention, though. No one has ever called me Miss Hopkins before.

Mr. Wills holds the general office door open and gestures for me to go inside. Then he leads me to his own office. I refuse to look at the secretary as I walk past, because she's probably gloating over by her computer.

When we're inside, he tells me to sit down and says he'll be back in a few minutes. I've never seen anything as depressing as Mr. Wills's office before. The walls are kind of khaki, and the curtains at the one window in the room are about the same, except where they've faded to something like the colour of dust. There are framed posters on the walls that are supposed to be motivating. One shows two cats up on a ladder, with their paws held up to the night sky. Underneath the ladder it reads, "Reach for the Stars." I guess that might get some people going.

There are two trophies on Mr. Wills's desk. One is for third prize in a curling bonspiel and the other is for surviving an ice fishing marathon. They're current, at least, not like the other trophies in the school. There's also a little Canadian flag beside them, and next to that, a picture of a woman with two children. He has it turned so he can see it, but the people sitting on the other side of the desk can see it too. I guess it's for appearances, but I can't imagine anyone being married to Mr. Wills. I wonder if he rented these people just for the picture taking.

I entertain myself like this for a while. It helps me feel like I'm clever enough to handle anything. After I've waited maybe five minutes, though, I stop feeling clever and start wondering if there's a remote camera in the room somewhere. Also if Mr. Wills is in the staff room right now, watching as I lose my nerve. I've put this stuff on my fingernails to keep me from biting them, so I can't do that any more. Instead, I chew on my bottom lip.

I don't know how long it is before Mr. Wills comes back, but when he does, he's carrying a tray with a teapot on it, two cups, no saucers, some packages of sugar, and little plastic containers with milk in them. Also a can of pop and an empty glass. There are two muffins on a plate and some white paper napkins from those shiny metal dispensers they have at ice cream stores.

"I didn't know if you liked tea," he says, "so I brought pop as well. The muffins are blueberry. My wife baked them and I brought them for lunch." Wow! Pop or tea? And muffins baked by his wife? So he actually has a real family, after all.

I'm sure Mr. Wills is expecting me to choose pop, so I do my usual contrary thing and ask for tea. With sugar, no milk. I sip a little and bite into the muffin, which is better than the ones we made in Foods. I'm wondering if his wife baked them so they'd coordinate with the secretary's nail polish, when Mr. Wills says, "I notice on your registration form that you want to be called Nell." He seems to be looking over my head at something in the corner of the room. "Is that right?"

"That's right," I say. "I'm named after Nellie McClung, but I prefer Nell." I'm a little surprised at myself for speaking up in a plain, strong way.

Mr. Wills nods. He has about half a muffin in his mouth and he swallows that loudly. "She was quite a woman. I hope you intend to follow in her footsteps."

"I don't," I say.

"What was it she said?" he goes on, like I hadn't just turned down the invitation. "'Never retreat, never explain, never apologize. Just get the job done and let them howl.'

Now there was a woman with a lot of spirit."

I've heard that quotation before, but I don't really see how if fits my circumstances. If I did make Shane howl, I'm certainly paying for it.

After a long pause, Mr. Wills says, "As I'm sure you're aware, I'm new at this school, so I didn't have the opportunity of meeting you and your uncle at Grade Seven Orientation last spring.

"I came with my mother," I say, but I give him major points for reading ALL of my registration form, and not just the top line.

"I thought ..."

"She's just away for a while," I tell him, hoping we can leave it at that.

We can. Mr. Wills nods again and doesn't ask any more about her. He slurps a little tea, then shifts in his chair and looks directly at me. I get the impression that the real interrogation is about to begin.

Instead, Mr. Wills asks, almost shyly, "I'd like to know if you feel safe in this school." I'm all tensed up, ready to defend myself. Then he comes up with a question like that!

I look down into my cup, and don't look up again. I suppose that's pretty much like a no.

After a while – and it feels like a long while – Mr. Wills says, "There is a lot I need to do to clean this school up, Nell. I don't want it to be a place where students who are good citizens are harassed by other students who ... perhaps aren't. But there's a procedure I have to follow in doing this.

And I need facts. I can't act on rumours, or second- or third-hand information."

Finally I get my eyes to move up and my mouth to open. "I thought Mr. Melnyk was supposed to be here," I squeak lamely.

"He's teaching," Mr. Wills says, "so he's not available. And I wanted to talk to you before the weekend." Then he tells me he's heard about Shane's behaviour toward me, but needs me to repeat the whole thing in my own words. I figure if he already knows it, it won't matter if I tell him about it again, so I do, but just about what happened in Foods.

Mr. Wills writes while I'm talking. Then he wants to know if there have been any more incidents. I say no. There's no point in mentioning what happened on the staircase, because Shane will just say that he protected me.

"No threats?" he asks. "No physical intimidation?"

I shake my head. Then he wants to know about Bonnie. He says Mr. Melnyk thinks she was threatening me when I was in his room during the Halloween dance.

"No," I say, "she was just trying to find out if I knew a friend of hers who lives in Beaumont." But I'm not the greatest liar in the world and I don't think he buys it.

He nods. His tea is all gone and he stirs in the empty cup with his spoon. "I can't put an end to the kind of intimidation that's going on at this school until people like you decide to work with me, Nell, but I promise you, I'm watching these events very carefully. Will you talk to Mr.

Melnyk or me if you have any further problems?" I tell him
I will, although I don't mean it, and then he lets me go.

I just have time to get to my locker, leave my coat, and
get my books. I arrive at my sixth period class, which is
Science, just as the late bell rings. We have a substitute
teacher, so we're watching a video. Lots of people whisper
and pass notes, but no one gets seriously out of hand. I kind
of nod off in my seat. Then it's time to go home.

When I get to my locker, Sam is waiting for me.

"I heard you were in the principal's office," he says.
"Did you ...?" He raises his eyebrows.

"No," I say, "I didn't tell him about Bonnie or any of the
rest of it. I just repeated what he already knew." I open my
locker.

"I wanted to warn you," Sam says. "Ziad thinks there
might be trouble over the weekend."

"Like I haven't already had it?" I demand. I slam my
locker door and click the lock, which is still one of the
school's. I haven't had time to change it.

"More trouble, then," Sam says. "Bonnie's saying things.
She may try something, so maybe you'll want to stay close to
home."

"I don't believe this!" I say. I'd throw my books again,
but I'm too tired to bend over and pick them up.

Sam says he'll walk to the end of the soccer field with
me if I want. The bus makes a loop at the end of the street
and then turns around. He's figured out that if we hurry, he
can get on at the 111th Avenue stop. Maybe he knew that

all the time and just wasn't sure he wanted to make the effort. Anyway, we leave school together.

I feel bad that I'm so snappy with him at times, so I try to make conversation. "What are you doing tomorrow?" I ask, like I'm interviewing him for TV.

"Going to school."

"Oh, I wish I could!" I say. I'm thinking he's made a joke.

"Really. I go to Islamic school on Saturdays."

I have enough sense not to tell him I feel sorry for him, but I do say, "That sounds like work."

Sam shrugs. "My parents send me to public school during the week so I can learn to be Canadian. On Saturday they make sure I don't forget where we came from. Fitting in is a lot of work."

"I guess I've never tried it."

"You fit in already," Sam says, "so you don't have to."

"Oh, right," I snort. "That's why Bonnie and Shane like me so much."

We get to his bus stop just as the bus is pulling up. "Good luck over the weekend," he says. "Ziad will be watching."

"Unfortunately, he's not the only one," I mutter to myself as the bus drives away. I wish all of my watchers would find something better to do.

Chapter Twelve

When I get to Mary Chase, and go inside to pick up my brother, there's so much activity I almost forget that Bonnie's loose somewhere and is supposed to be stalking me. Kids are stacking chairs and dusting shelves. Four or five move around the room picking up bits of crayon and lint from the rug with loops of masking tape. Every time they fill up the sticky side of their loop, they call out to Mrs. Montcrieff, "Another one, please. This one's done." I've never seen students get excited about picking up carpet lint before, but I guess if you're a teacher at Mary Chase, you have to be able to make things like that happen.

When Mikey sees me at the door, he runs over. "We've got four boxes of books," he says. "The whole school is helping now!" The way he's dancing around, I think for a minute that he has to go to the bathroom, but he settles down when Mrs. Montcrieff joins us, so I guess that isn't the reason.

"Your brother has really started something," she says. "When the children in this class found out about the school your mother and the other peacekeepers are fixing up, they all wanted to help. Besides those books, we have boxes of paper and pencils and crayons. And now they want to write letters to everyone at Camp Grey Wolf. And to the students in the village school.

While we're talking, Mikey loses interest in the conversation and goes back to rummage through the boxes of books. Maybe he's counting them or just feeling pleased about how many there are. Mrs. Montcrieff sort of tugs at me to step outside the classroom. Then she says, "This is the best thing in the world for Lester B. – now he can focus on the good your mother's doing and not be obsessed with the risks she's taking by being there."

Maybe Mrs. Montcrieff thinks I look doubtful, because then she says, "Things are getting better, Nell. Cheer up."

I do that, of course. Right away. I'm so cheered up that by the time we get home I tell Mikey to get his own snack, then I step out of my clothes, leave them in a pile on the floor, put on my pajamas, and get into bed. In a while Mikey comes into my room and tells me that there's a new e-mail from our mother, but it has PRIVATE on the subject line. He wants to know what that means. Of course he knows perfectly well.

When Uncle Martin agreed to let us use his e-mail account, we promised that we would not try to read any letter marked PRIVATE. He can tell if it's been opened before he reads it, and he said if we did that even once, he'd change his e-mail address so we couldn't use it any more. I remind Mikey of that and tell him to leave the letter alone. Then I roll over and continue with my plan to drop out of the human race.

Mikey and Uncle Martin do all the cooking and table setting for dinner. They really don't have any choice, since I'm playing dead in the bedroom. And what I hear and smell makes me think they're fixing something Italian. Mikey is even trying to sing along in his reedy little voice, so they seem to be having a good time.

When dinner is ready, Uncle Martin knocks on my door and then comes into the room. I don't look at him, but I can tell he's doing something with my clothes because I hear his breath woosh out when he bends over to pick them up. And then I hear a sort of rustling sound as he folds them and puts them somewhere – probably on the chair beside the dresser.

"Can you come to the table, Nell?" he asks. "I'd prefer it. Unless you're too sick to move. In that case we'd better think about going to the medicentre."

"I can move," I say, "but I'm not too sure about the eating part."

"Maybe just a little pasta," Uncle Martin says. "No red sauce. Just a little olive oil, salt, and garlic."

Normally, I would not get up from my deathbed for

that. But I don't want to go to the doctor and hear that what's wrong with me is all in my head, so I put on my bathrobe. It, by the way, isn't in much better shape than the one Uncle Martin wears or the one he donated to the Clifford costume. Then I go to the table.

*M*aybe I'm not really sick with bubonic plague or anything like that, but I truly don't have an appetite. I pick a little at the spaghetti, but I certainly don't get into eating it the way Mikey does. This is spaghetti from an Italian grocery store, of course, and each piece is about a metre long and covered in some kind of sticky red sauce Uncle Martin's made according to his own private recipe.

Mikey isn't wigging out over the food, probably because he's having so much fun with it. He skewers a strand of it with his fork, puts it in his mouth, then sucks and sucks until he gets to the end of it. There's always a little pop when the tail end of a spaghetti strand disappears into his mouth. After a while he has lots of snaky little red marks on his cheeks where spaghetti tails have flipped around just before he finishes them off.

Uncle Martin is surprisingly laid back about Mikey's eating display. In fact, he gets pretty carried away himself. It's obvious he believes he's mastered the fine art of spaghetti eating. He twirls his fork around and around on his plate until he's wound the length of the living room onto it. Then he puts the whole load in his mouth and chews heartily.

He's turned a little pink from the effort, and by now Mikey looks like he has red tattoos all over his face.

Normally I'd find all this foodishness kind of disgusting, but tonight I don't have anything to say to either one of them. I just put in my time drinking the peppermint tea Uncle Martin has made for me. I don't really like it, but I drink it anyway because I don't want to make a fuss. I just want to get my public appearance over with, go back to bed, and be left alone.

When the spaghetti show dies down, though, Uncle Martin pushes back from the table a little and announces that he has two things to tell us. "Your mother won't be able to call you tomorrow night," he says. I guess that's the first thing.

"Why not?" Mikey says and his cheeks and eyes start to crumple into each other.

"Something has come up at the base," Uncle Martin tells him, "and she won't be able to make the call. She says she'll keep trying. Maybe she can do it on Sunday." Mikey doesn't look happy, but there isn't any further crumpling, so that's one crisis avoided.

Uncle Martin's news doesn't break my heart, because I wasn't counting on the phone call. But I would like to hear Mom's voice – without the army boots and the chevrons and the C-7 rifle. That's not quite the truth. I'd actually LOVE to hear just my own mother's voice, like she was here and belonged to us again.

But there were two things Uncle Martin wanted to tell us. That was just the first. The second is that Christine Stuart is coming for dinner tomorrow night. We're apparently supposed to get very excited about this, and Uncle Martin is definitely not pleased with our response.

"Who's Christine Stuart?" Mikey wants to know.

"The woman who ruined your day," I say. "Remember? You thought she was Emily Carr, and she told you Alice was dead." That's mean and jealous, but sometimes I can be.

"She said she WAS Emily Carr!" Mikey wails. He runs to the back door and stands there like he's threatening to put on his coat and boots and disappear into the snow to the sound of howling wolves. It doesn't have much effect though, because the weather's still very mild. He could stay outside for hours and not have much more than cold feet and a dripping nose.

"Mike!" Uncle Martin says, and it begins to look like we're off on another Kielbasa Episode. But Uncle Martin stays in his chair. "Christine was just doing the job she was hired to do that day. And she feels very badly that you were scared. That's why I've invited her for dinner. She wants to know how you're doing." Mikey comes back from the door with his head down and leans on the refrigerator.

"And how you are too, Nell," Uncle Martin says. "I thought you'd both be pleased." He looks a little pouty himself at this point.

I should have known something was going on. Uncle Martin hasn't played his usual Beatles music in the shower the last few mornings. He's played The Traveling Wilburys

– Traveling Willow Babies, I call them. George Harrison is part of the group and he's a former Beatle, but it's still a big change in routine. I'm not very sharp these days or I would have picked it up.

I also would have put away the notes from Sam and Shane, which I suddenly realize are still where I left them at noon – crumpled up in between the salt and pepper shakers. I reach out quickly, grab them and put them in the pocket of my bathrobe.

"What's that, Nell?" Uncle Martin asks.

"Just some notes about homework," I say. He looks at me very hard. Then he looks away and down at his plate. Finally he says, "From the look on your face, this homework must be very important to you."

"It is very important," I say, but I know he doesn't believe me. Uncle Martin may not be clued in about kids at home, but he sure knows how they behave in school. He's just caught me with two little scraps of paper I don't want him to see. Most teachers take notes like these and read them out. Even Mr. Melnyk has done that once or twice, and he's the closest thing to Mother Theresa we have at JAWS.

But Uncle Martin just asks, "Are you feeling well enough to do your homework?"

"I'm going to try," I say.

"Well," he says, "I guess you'd better get to it." He gives me another long look. Then he carries his plate and glass to the dishwasher, puts them in and goes downstairs. Suddenly it's a little chilly in the kitchen.

Mikey's pretty quiet for the rest of the evening. By about 7:00 he wants to get into bed with me, so we read a lot of his books together. Then he wants to write a letter to Bosnia – specifically to the little kid with the orange jacket who won't talk to anybody. "Edin," I tell him. "The kid's name is Edin."

Mikey wants help with his letter writing, though, so I stay in bed and call across the hall to him about things he can say. "Tell him about your school," or "Tell him how you sometimes take Denver for a walk." Things like that.

"He won't know who that is," Mikey says.

"Tell him," I say. "Describe how he looks." I surprise myself by actually getting into the whole thing. Why should that be surprising, though? Sometimes I can make an effort.

Pretty soon I hear the printer going. Then Mikey's in the bathroom, brushing his teeth. He comes to my door and asks me to tuck him in, which I get up and do. I brush my teeth myself and then I go in to check that he's turned the computer off. He hasn't.

My brother Mikey is a very smart little kid. He knows all about computers – actually more than I do. But one thing he doesn't quite understand is that Uncle Martin can tell if we open his private letters before he does, but he can't tell if we open them again after he has. Maybe he could if he had an army intelligence computer, but he can't on the set-up he's got in this house.

So instead of turning off the computer, I decide to check out what the PRIVATE message from Mom is all about. I imagine it's more talk about me and I figure I have a right to know what she and Uncle Martin are saying. I wish now that I'd hadn't read it, but it's too late to change that.

Subject: **For Martin Mackelwain – PRIVATE**
Date: November 3, 2000 23:03:15
From: "MCpl.AS.Mackelwain,ASU Edmonton, 582-5418,0900" <mail466@dnd.ca>
To: mmackelwain@hotmail.com

Dear Martin,

There's been a tragic accident here. I don't know how to tell Nell and Lester B. about it yet, but I need to let you know that I can't phone on Saturday, as I told them I would.

This morning two young brothers were taking a shortcut over a field near their home. One was five and the other was seven. I've mentioned them to Nell and Lester B. In fact the children at Mary Chase have started sending letters for me to give to the younger one whose name is Edin. Edin Hidic. His name was Edin Hidic, I should say.

We've talked and talked to people around V.K. about walking only on marked paths, but this morning the two brothers went off on their own for some reason. Edin is dead. His brother Mirsad will live, but has lost one of his legs below the knee.

Martin, we're all devastated. It's hard to accept that these children can be in such danger all the time and yet have done nothing to deserve it. The chaplain on the base is holding a special service at about the time I had signed up to call you and I feel I have to go – partly for the others, and partly for myself.

I'll keep trying for a later call on Saturday. There's one person who might trade me her time slot if I can get her something she wants from town. Elvis says he'll go into V.K. for me. I'll reach you on the weekend somehow, even if I have to call in the middle of the night here to do it.

I finally got an e-mail from Nell but it was obviously written just so she could say she'd done it. I can't help thinking there's something serious bothering her, in addition to the fact that I'm her mother. I know you feel you don't have the right touch to get her to open up, but I think if you really try, you can. Are you taking her rejections seriously? You shouldn't. She's young and confused. You're the adult.

Thinking of you all with much love,

Aly
"MCpl.AS.Mackelwain,ASU Edmonton,582-5418,0900"
e-mail:466@dnd.ca

After I read the letter, I sit at the computer a long time. At first I think it will hurt me to move. Then I think it will hurt more if I don't. I turn off everything I can put my hands on. I'm cold, even inside my bathrobe, so I wrap a blanket around my shoulders. I walk into the kitchen and look out the French doors at the night sky. The moon's riding over the tip of the garage, but it isn't full. It's tiny and sharp and has no face at all.

Chapter Thirteen

When I get up on Saturday, I'm worried that Uncle Martin will want to have another heart-to-heart talk. I don't feel like I can handle that. But he acts quite stand-offish the whole day, and is mostly into work. I didn't clean up the dishes last night, so there's that to do and I suppose he doesn't appreciate it. Then there's the usual Saturday routine. I scrub both bathrooms, and Mikey cleans his room and sweeps the kitchen. Uncle Martin vacuums and cleans with this feathery little blue thing that's supposed to have a magnetic attraction for dust.

Usually I take Mikey to the library in the afternoon so Uncle Martin can have some time to himself, but today he takes Mikey to the store and leaves me home. He doesn't even ask if I want to go along. That stings a little. His silence isn't so much saying he doesn't believe me, as it is telling me he's forgotten I exist. I'm starting to know how my mother feels about the way I've cut her out of my life.

*A*fter Uncle Martin and Mikey get back from the store, there's more kitchen work – peeling and slicing and cooking something that smells kind of like fish and kind of like aging broccoli. I try my best to breathe through my mouth and dig into the pile of homework that's building up. We may not have exciting assignments at JAWS, but we have a lot of them.

Mikey decides to watch all his Clifford videos back to back – something our mother would never let him do in a million years if she was here. He checks in with me on one of his bathroom breaks. He's wearing a blue bandana handkerchief over his nose to protect it from kitchen smells and his eyes are a little bleary from too much non-stop video watching, but he seems happy. He whispers to me that Uncle Martin has promised he can have macaroni and cheese for dinner if he doesn't say anything about the food while Christine's here. At least one of us is still in our uncle's good books.

I don't know what to do about Mikey's letter to Edin. I can't tell my brother that a kid younger than he is – one he's started to care about – has died in an unbelievably horrible way. In the first place I'm not supposed to know. And in the second place, I don't think Mikey can handle it. I'm not even handling it very well myself. Every time I think about this innocent little boy getting blown up just because he ran across a field, I start to blubber. There are splotches all over the paragraph I'm trying to write.

It's my last chance to convince people that matches are one of the ten things we need to take with us to our desert island. A guy named Ben Sanders insists he can make fire by striking stones together, so matches aren't essential. And if we take them, it means we have to leave out something else that is.

Karen Lavoie is ready to abandon me and my matches because of his argument, but I don't think he knows what he's talking about. You can't just pick up any old pair of rocks, bang them together, and get the kind of sparks that make fire. I'm pretty sure what you need is flint, and there's no guarantee it will be on hand when you need it.

Let's just suppose Ben Sanders can really do what he says he can, though. He might die at any time on our imaginary island, and if he's the only one who knows how to get a fire going, we'll be in trouble. He could teach the skill to someone else right away, of course. Then we'd always have a fire builder around. But he might just as easily keep his knowledge to himself. Some people do bad things with power. Just look at Shane, if you need an example. Or Bonnie. Let's not forget her.

I guess my biggest problem with Ben's idea is that I don't like relying on other people. Mom's always bragged to her friends that I've practically raised myself. If I have, it's because people aren't reliable. ESPECIALLY adults. I still remember how Mikey stood at the door and cried for our father after he left. I might even have cried myself. I can't recall. And now, when it's obvious I can't get out of this mess alone, Mom's gone too. Doesn't that prove I shouldn't have needed anyone in the first place?

A s you can imagine, my paragraph writing doesn't get very far. I can't come up with anything new, so I finally decide just to repeat all the arguments for matches I've used already. Every time I start to put words down, though, I see this little kid running off somewhere to play. Then there's an explosion and he's gone. I can't get the picture out of my head. After a while it's Mikey who's running – down the street toward Mary Chase. I rest my head on the desk and wait for the next explosion.

I wish I could tell someone about Edin. I'd phone Sam, if I could. I know he's just another kid with no power, like me, but somehow I think he'd understand.

C hristine gets to the house about six. We hear her before we see her. We hear her car, I mean. It must be pretty old, because it sounds like loose nuts and bolts are banging against the hood as she drives up in front of the house. Uncle Martin lets her in and Mikey and I straggle out to say hello.

I've been in my bathrobe all day, but I manage to put on jeans and a blue sweater just before she arrives. When he sees me doing that, Mikey decides to wear a necktie with his

Clifford T-shirt. He knots it himself. It looks kind of accidental, but I think it shows that we've both made an effort. Still, we probably look kind of stressed. My eyes are all puffed up and Mikey's are a little red from his video marathon.

Christine is almost glamorous, though, especially compared to the way she looked when we saw her last. She's wearing makeup and her hair is scrunched and fluffy instead of matted down from wearing Emily Carr's hairnet all day. Her pants and sweater are black, and she has a white silk scarf draped around her neck and shoulders. It's the kind Snoopy wears when he's reliving his World War I pilot days, only longer.

"How are you, Lester B.?" she asks. "Or should I call you Mike?" She bends over a little and holds out her hand. He shakes it kind of awkwardly, but his eyes are soft when he looks at Christine, and I can tell he isn't upset with her any more.

"You can call me Lester B. if you want to," he says. That confirms what I just said.

Then Christine turns to me. "Nell," she says and smiles. I guess she takes a second look, though, because she kind of grabs back the breath she's just let out. "Is something wrong?" she asks. "Are you ill?"

"I'm not sure," I say, and then her face and Uncle Martin's and Mikey's and even my mother's start swirling around me. Everyone seems to be speaking some language I've never heard before. I keel over.

I think Uncle Martin's notion of a quiet dinner where Mikey and I act civilized pretty well goes out the window after that. By the time I can sort out all their faces and I'm back in the room enough to know that my mom's isn't one of them, I'm lying on the couch. Uncle Martin is holding something I can see through and bending over me. Mikey is fanning my feet with a folded up magazine. Tears roll down his face and he's crying, "Don't die, Nellie! Don't leave me here!" Christine has her arms around Mikey and is saying or singing something into the top of his head.

Uncle Martin holds out the see-through thing, which turns out to be a glass of water, and talks to me. At first I think he's speaking that new language again. Then I finally realize he's saying, "Drink this, Nell," which isn't really that complex, and I try to. I spill some down my neck until I get the hang of it, and after that it's like I've been drinking water out of glasses all my life.

Uncle Martin and Christine discuss what they should do next. He's flustered and wants to rush me to the medi-centre, if it's still open. Otherwise, he says we'll go to Emergency at the Royal Alec Hospital. Christine, it turns out, is used to medical emergencies. Her mother is a nurse. She tells Uncle Martin to calm down. "Let's not rush into anything yet," she says. "As long as she's awake and warm, it's better to keep her here a while and watch her carefully."

"Are you sure?" Uncle Martin asks.

Christine smiles and nods. "That's what we'll end up doing at the hospital. At least in your house, we can try to make ourselves comfortable. You know what lineups at Emergency are like."

"Exactly what are we watching for?" Uncle Martin wants to know.

Christine shrugs. "How long ago did she eat?" She really does have a nice voice. I could listen to it for hours.

"I'm not sure." Of course Uncle Martin's not sure. He's been ignoring me all day.

Christine asks me, and I admit that I haven't. Eaten, I mean. Not today, anyway. She clucks her tongue and Uncle Martin looks sheepish. The way they're acting, like an old married couple, I wonder if they've been meeting secretly for coffee every day since the whole Emily Carr episode took place.

"Food may be all she needs," Christine says. "Let's just eat on TV trays in the living room so Nell can stay on the couch."

Mikey jumps up and down. "Hooray," he says, flashing the empty space he's got reserved for his new teeth.

"I'm afraid I don't have any TV trays," Uncle Martin says. Mikey slumps down disappointed on the rug and Christine looks at him like he's just told her he has only three toes on each foot. But she doesn't give up.

She finds a regular tea tray somewhere in the back of the cupboard for me. She sets a place for Mikey on the coffee table, and she and Uncle Martin hold their plates in their laps. Christine ends up eating macaroni and cheese with Mikey and me, while Uncle Martin kind of keeps his plate to himself. Whatever he's eating doesn't smell much any more, but it still looks suspicious.

Everyone has something red to drink in glasses with stems – fruit juice for Mikey and me, and I suppose wine for the adults. I've got a couple of soft pillows at my back, and a dark green afghan tucked around me. I'm feeling warm and protected and I'm having a really nice time. So is Mikey. He tells Christine, "I just love picnics. I wish we could eat like this every day."

Christine talks to us a little about her family. She says she was born in a little town called Loch something where the streets are made of brick and stone. "Like King Arthur?" Mikey wants to know.

"Wrong country," Christine says, "but the royalty part fits." Mikey smiles. He LOVES it when he thinks he's got something right.

Where Christine grew up, she says, almost everyone lives on one hill or another and all the kids have a long hike down to school every day and then up again at night. She doesn't exactly say she walked on snow as high as the fence tops, but it's that kind of story. I don't mind, though, and Mikey doesn't seem to either. As for Uncle Martin, he just looks kind of spaced out and comfortable.

After a bit he and Christine take away the dishes and start cleaning up the kitchen. I can hear her trying to teach him a Scottish song. Uncle Martin's voice is very low, and while I wouldn't say he should audition for the Edmonton Opera, he manages to sing the right notes. Christine sings along with him for a while, then she starts to whistle. Mikey runs into the kitchen when he hears her and whistles too, which leaves me lying on the front couch alone. I don't like how that feels, so I go into the kitchen as well. When I start to sing, Christine's face lights up. "Ah," she says, "a wee soprano."

After that, I really get into singing, and the sounds coming out of my mouth kind of take on a life of their own. I don't know if you can imagine how that feels. I'm not sure I can describe it, either, except to say that I'd almost forgotten I had a voice for anything but being scared, or angry, or trying to protect myself. Now, I remember that I do. It feels kind of important.

When we're finished in the kitchen, Uncle Martin invites Christine to come down to the basement. "Let me show you the bachelor quarters I've set up down there," he says. I think he's making a joke, but I still can't tell with him.

"I'd like to help Nell settle in on the couch first," Christine says. She fluffs my pillows and tucks the afghan around me. Then she sits next to me. "That's better," she says. She looks at my face for a while, which ought to make me uncomfortable, but doesn't. Then she asks, "You don't have Martin's eyes, or your brother's. Are they like your mother's?"

"People say I have my father's eyes," I answer back. "Unfortunately."

"Why unfortunately? Your eyes are beautiful."

"You think so?" I ask. I want to be sure I've heard her correctly.

"I do. They're full of ..."

"Speckles." I finish her sentence for her. For a moment I thought she'd seen something special about me.

"No, sparkles," she says. "They could be sunlight. Or starlight. But you have whole galaxies in your eyes, Nell. Have you never noticed that before?"

"Never," I say, but I try to make room for myself in the picture she's painting.

Uncle Martin and Mikey have been hanging around by the doorway into the kitchen, like what's happening between Christine and me is personal, and they don't know if they should come into the living room or not. After she kisses me on the top of the head, she goes to stand with them.

"Will you be all right here, Nell?" Uncle Martin asks.

"Sure," I say. At that moment I feel like it's true.

He and Christine turn to leave, but Mikey goes on standing there. "Coming with us?" Uncle Martin asks him.

"No," Mikey says. He walks over and sits beside me on the couch. "I'm going to stay here and look after my sister." He's a funny little guy.

Chapter Fourteen

*I*t's nice having a woman in the house – not like having our own mother home and safe, but it's still nice. And it feels good knowing that Mikey's hanging around because he cares, and Christine and Uncle Martin are just downstairs and they'll probably check on me in a while. I'm thinking maybe it's not the worst thing in the world to depend on your family, even if they are a little out of the ordinary. I'm lying on the couch, drifting along in this warm, safe bubble, when Mikey, who's standing by the front window, says, "There's someone outside looking at our house."

My eyes fly open. "By the tree, you mean?" I'm remembering how I thought I saw someone in the shadow of the spruce tree on Halloween night.

"No," Mikey says. "Across the street."

"Don't just stand there, then!" I hiss. "Get down!"

Mikey drops to his knees and peeks through the Norfolk pine Uncle Martin keeps in a pot in front of the window.

I raise my head and shoulders and scrunch back against the arm of the couch. "Is it a girl or a guy?" Then right away,

I tell myself it's a useless question, because Bonnie looked like a boy to me the first time I saw her.

"It's a boy. He's coming across to our side of the street now and ... he's waving." Mikey stands up and waves back.

By now I'm on the floor beside my little brother and I pull him back down again. "What did you do that for?"

"He was waving."

"You don't wave to people just because they wave to you!"

In a moment I hear steps on the front porch and a quiet knock at the door. Mikey looks at me.

"Don't move!" I tell him. I hold my breath and count in my head to eight. Then the knock comes again. I crawl to the door, then stand up and try to see who it is out the peek hole. It doesn't work any better now than it did on Halloween. All I can see is that someone who looks like he has a black cushion on top of his head is standing outside the door.

"Nell Hawkins?" the cushion-head says. "Are you in there?"

I don't make a peep. Neither does Mikey, although he's standing so close up against me that I feel claustrophobic.

"Nell Hawkins?" the cushion-head says again.

It's the name that finally gets to me. "It's HOPKINS," I say, trying to sound fierce. "And you should know that I'm not alone. What do you want?"

"I'm Methael's brother."

"Who's Methael?" Mikey whispers.

"I don't know," I whisper back. "Who's Methael?" I repeat out loud.

"I mean Sam. Sorry," he says. "You're his friend, so I thought you'd know his ... I'm Sam's brother, Ziad."

I open the door just a crack and peek out. The guy standing in the doorway is not fat exactly, but big like a wrestler. He's wearing jeans and a plaid jacket with a peaky black toque on his head. I've probably seen him around and didn't know he was anybody special.

"Hi," he says. "You're Nell." I nod, although it isn't exactly a question. "Hi," he says to Mikey, who also nods. "You haven't had any trouble today, have you?"

"Ever since I got up," I say.

Ziad looks blank for a moment. Maybe he thinks I'm a little dense, because then he says more slowly, "Any trouble with BONNIE, I mean."

"No."

"Who's Bonnie?" Mikey wants to know.

"Good." Ziad says. "I was afraid she'd try something."

I've never had a bodyguard before, so I don't know exactly how to act or what to say. Then there's the problem of Mikey, squeezing the circulation out of my hand.

"If you need anything, you can call me on my cell," Ziad says. He's talking right at me, now – handing me a card. "Because I promised Sam I'd watch out for you."

I look at the card. There's a lightning bolt down the side, with a big Z beside it, and a phone number.

"Why do you have a cell phone?" Mikey asks suspiciously. "Are you a drug dealer?"

Ziad laughs, and doesn't seem offended. "No," he says.

"My cousin's husband had an accident, so he can't work, or get around. I take orders for her pita bread and deliver it to her customers."

I guess doing good deeds runs in Sam's family.

When Uncle Martin gets around, he bumps into things, and I can usually hear him coming and get prepared. Even when he's in his stocking feet and thinks he's being extra quiet, the bones in his toes crack and give him away. So I jump when I hear his voice behind me now, and Ziad and Mikey do too. "What is it, Nell?" Uncle Martin says. He comes right up to the door and pulls it completely open. "Is there a problem?"

"N-no," I stammer. Then all in one breath I say, "This is the brother of someone I know at school. His name is Ziad. Not the person I know at school, I mean. His name is Sam. Or that's what people call him. This is Ziad. He's Sam's brother. Sam is in my Foods class." Uncle Martin narrows his eyes and I imagine Ziad gets the feeling he isn't really welcome.

"I just stopped by because I wanted to know if your daughter was all right, sir," he says. "My brother asked me to." He keeps his head down when he talks, like there's a new person wearing the crown in England, and that person is Uncle Martin.

"His niece," I say. "This is my UNCLE Martin."

"I apologize," Ziad says. He shifts his weight back and forth on his feet and rubs his hands together. "You have a nice house here, sir."

"Thank you."

"Well." Ziad holds onto the rail and backs down the steps. "I was just checking to see if your ... if Nell is all right."

"Is there any reason why she shouldn't be?" Uncle Martin asks in his teacher-detective voice.

"It's just ... something from school," Ziad says. I imagine he's wishing he'd never knocked on the door. "Sir, I ... I'm sorry to disturb the peace of your house." He kind of bows to my uncle, and then he's gone. Not exactly like Zorro, but the empty sidewalk takes over pretty quickly once he's made up his mind to go.

Uncle Martin shuts the door and turns to look at me. Christine, who's apparently been sitting on the couch with Mikcy and listening, says, "What on earth?" but Uncle Martin is suddenly very much in charge.

"Nell," he says, "I think you have some things you'd like to tell us."

*I*n the old days I wouldn't have talked about what's been going on in my life to anyone except my mother. Sometimes not even to her. I think I've made that very clear. But a lot has happened to me lately. And Christine is a very reassuring person. I've liked her from the minute I met her, even if I was a little jealous when it began to look like she and Uncle Martin were getting cozy with each other. Now I get this little flutter in my stomach that moves up into my throat, and when it gets to my mouth, I open it and the whole story comes out.

While I'm talking, I'm aware that Mikey's there and that he really shouldn't be listening to this. I mention that to Uncle Martin. But Mikey blurts out, "Nell's my sister and I'm not leaving!" so he gets to hear a lot that little kids shouldn't know about.

Of course Uncle Martin asks to see the notes. "I don't know what I did with them," I tell him.

"You put them in your bathrobe pocket," he says. "Aren't they still there?" I told you Uncle Martin is wise about notes and stuff like that.

I go and dig them out. He looks them over. "Sam's the boy in your Foods class?" he asks.

"Yes," I say. "Ziad's his brother. Sam's the only friend I've got at that rotten school."

Then Uncle Martin reads the one from Bonnie, courtesy of Shane. "This is a threat," he says. "How do you know it's not serious? Why didn't you tell me?"

"I didn't know how," I say. I hang my head like I'm ashamed, but I don't think that's exactly why I'm doing it.

"I suppose your mother was right," Uncle Martin says. "I should have done a better job of encouraging you to talk."

"She probably wasn't ready, Martin," Christine says.

"It's okay," I tell them both. "Sam told me his brother was looking out for me, but I didn't know if I could trust him. Now it looks like I can, maybe Bonnie will leave me alone."

"And when he's not?" Uncle Martin asks. He's starting to pink up now, and there's an edge to his voice. "If this Ziad is on your side because of his brother, he can just as well be off your side for some similar reason, can't he?"

"Martin," Christine says, very soothing and low.

Mikey's been puttering around by the Norfolk pine again. Now he cries, "Look! There's someone out there!" He drops to the floor and I jump out of my skin.

Uncle Martin walks to the window and looks out. "Mike," he says. "It's just Mr. Lapinski across the street walking Denver." He waves and then pulls the curtain closed. "Is there some reason why we have to live in a fishbowl?" he mutters.

He walks over to the armchair near the window and motions for Mikey to come and sit down next to him. Mikey sits down on the floor beside Christine instead. "I'm just trying to take care of my sister," he says. His fists are balled up in his lap and he looks very grim. For some reason that kind of cuts me up.

"All I'm trying to say," Uncle Martin goes on, looking even grimmer, "is that this is a democracy. We can't rely on people like Ziad to keep us safe. We have laws and a justice system to do that."

"So what does that mean?" I ask. I'm sitting on the floor with Christine now, too. I suppose it's unfair to Uncle Martin that we're all clumped up together and he's alone, but that's what's happened. Mikey is holding my hand and Christine has her arms around both of us.

"It means, Nell, that you have to have the courage not to be intimidated. It means you have to speak up. And it means that on Monday morning, you and I are going to school together to see the principal. What's his name?"

"Mr. Wills," I say. "He's going to think I'm a liar." Uncle Martin shrugs. "Anyway," I go on, "he can't do anything. He's been asking for MY help, so that should tell you how much control he has of the situation."

"If you spoke to the principal," Uncle Martin says very quietly, "I should have known about it." I don't offer to help out with the silence after that and neither does anyone else. He stands up. "I'll see his secretary on Monday morning and make an appointment."

"I don't think you'll like her," I tell him.

Uncle Martin sighs as if he's surrounded by fools. "I don't see what that has to do with anything."

I hate to admit it, but he's probably right. The real question I need to be thinking about is what I'll say in Mr. Wills's office on Monday. When I was in the kitchen and I was thinking how good it felt to have my voice back, I meant my singing voice. I wasn't thinking about my speaking-up voice, which I'm not sure I had in the first place. I know I always used to tell the truth, but I'm not sure I'm brave enough to do that any more.

Chapter Fifteen

Mikey spends Sunday morning trying to take care of me. He brings me tea and burnt toast about nine o'clock. The tea's a little sweet, maybe, but I drink it. At least it's not peppermint. I also eat the toast. I really don't have much choice, since Mikey hangs around wanting to know if everything is all right and if I need anything. I figure, what's a little sugar and charcoal in your system compared to brotherly love and all that?

When I don't need anything else and no one tries to storm our house and kidnap me by noon, Mikey gets bored and goes across the street to visit Denver. Just after he leaves, a call comes through from Mom. Uncle Martin answers the phone down in the basement and yells up the stairs right away that it's her.

I've already said that by now I'm ready to talk to my mother, but I still don't have anything very brilliant to say when I pick up the phone except, "Hello."

"Nellie?" Mom says. Then she corrects herself. "Nell?" Her voice is kind of spidery and doesn't even sound like hers. "Are you all right?"

"I'm all right," I say. Then I hear these muffled, raspy sounds coming from her side of the receiver. It's not like static or what they call a bad connection, and I'm shocked when I realize that my mom is crying – or trying not to. I don't think I've ever heard her do that before, and right away I'm trying not to cry along with her.

"I know it's hard about the little boy, Mom," I say with my voice and my heart jumping up and down. "I'm sorry."

"The little boy?" she asks like she isn't sure who I mean. Then she says, "Oh. Martin told you. I wish he hadn't. It's ... yes, it's very hard. It's ..." She pauses. "But I'm not talking about that, Nell. I'm talking about the things that are happening to you at school. I got Martin's e-mail about it this morning. I haven't been able to get on the phone before now."

"Oh," I say. "I didn't know he'd told you." I can't really add anything noble like, "It's not important," or "I can look after myself." I want to be a hero and say that, but what's happening to me IS important. Also, I've told you how I hate admitting it, but I don't think I can manage on my own.

"I shouldn't have asked you to go to that school," Mom says. "Especially when you didn't want to. I'm sorry I didn't listen. But Nell? Will you listen to me now?"

"I'm listening."

"You don't have to stay. You can leave tomorrow and go to the academic challenge program if you want to."

"It's probably too late to get in."

"You can try, though. Check it out. Martin will check it out for you, if you ask him."

"What about Mikey? You said he needs me near by so he can get away from school at lunch and come home earlier in the afternoon."

"Your brother will be fine. I'm more worried about you right now than I am about him. He can go to Happy Gardens for lunch."

"Jolly."

"You don't think it's a good idea?"

"I mean it's Jolly Gardens, Mom. Not Happy." I laugh. My mother is not too good with details.

"Jolly Gardens, then," she says. Now we're both laughing together, just like we used to.

"He'll hate the idea," I say.

"But he can make the adjustment," Mom says. "I think we've protected him too much and expected too much from you." I admit that's how it's felt to me. I feel better hearing her say it out loud.

Mom's voice is pretty much back to normal now, but she keeps on apologizing and assuring me that I have choices and don't have to be miserable.

"Mom," I finally cut in, "it's okay. You don't have to keep saying you're sorry, because ..." Now I'm choking up again, and I need to clear my throat a few times. "Because I'm proud of you, Mom," I say eventually. "And I'm sorry, too."

Mikey comes in then. I tell him it's Mom and give him

the phone right away. He woofs into the receiver a couple of times. Then he says hello in his human voice and tells her he's on the job. That's actually what he says. "Don't worry, Mom, I'm on the job. I've been across the street pretending to play with Denver, but I've really been watching our house to make sure that Bonnie girl doesn't come here and try to beat Nellie up."

He's still assuring Mom that he'll stay on the job as long as it takes, when her fifteen minutes is up and the line goes dead. For a while he keeps shouting things over the dial tone – about the book collecting and all the letters his class is writing. Most of it he's already e-mailed her about. He hangs up the phone, but then picks it up again. "I forgot," he says. "A peacekeeper is coming to my school on Remembrance Day!" He barks a few times, then hangs up again and races to turn the computer on. He's only seven years old, but he's already figured out that e-mails can almost travel at the speed of speech.

Mom's phone call doesn't charge me up like it does Mikey. Hearing her voice makes me want to reach out and touch her, and of course I can't. I feel very sad that she's so far away. I'm not sure if sadness is easier to live with than anger, or not. I fall asleep on the couch and don't wake up until the phone rings again.

It's Christine. She tells me that Tuesday she's going into rehearsal for a musical version of *Through the Looking Glass.*

She's the bloodthirsty queen who keeps yelling, "Off with their heads" all the time.

"I should have mentioned this to you before," she says. "It's good to have the work, and I need the money. But we put in ten-hour days during rehearsal, and I won't always be able to stay in touch. Leave a message on my answering machine if you need to talk, though, and I'll get back to you as soon as I can."

"I'm going to be all right," I tell her. "I don't think you need to worry." I figure if I tell people that enough times, I may start to believe it myself.

Maybe it's because the phone wakes me up the second time it rings, but I catch myself hoping it's Sam. I need to talk to someone about Edin, and there's no one except Mom who knows that I know. If I could just say, "This awful thing happened and it's not right!" to someone who cared, I think I'd feel better. I know Sam isn't supposed to call me, but I just ... hoped for a minute that he had. Hope doesn't have to be reasonable, does it?

I go on feeling sad for the rest of the day, but Mikey's in a good space. He only gets in a tiny snit when Uncle Martin tells him he'll have to stay at school for lunch tomorrow. "It's in order to protect Nell," Uncle Martin says. "It could be dangerous for her to come home in the middle of the day."

Mikey gets a very serious look on his face after Uncle

Martin says this. He nods and pats my hand. Uncle Martin is starting to get the hang of parenting. If we stay around long enough, he may even be eligible for Uncle of the Year.

Chapter Sixteen

Monday is Day Two of JAWS' famous four-day week. That means Bonnie's suspension is over today. I mention this to Uncle Martin as I get out of the car. He's driven me all the way to school and is going in to talk to Mr. Wills's secretary.

I'm not expecting to see Sam today, but I'm pleased that he's waiting for me when I get to my locker. He says he's worried that Ziad's visit got me in trouble. "In a way it did," I say. I explain that Uncle Martin ended up finding out everything that's been happening at school. "He's in the office right now," I go on, "making an appointment to see Mr. Wills."

Sam leans against the wall by my locker, looking like he's let me down or something. "Maybe you should have told the whole truth in the first place," he says.

"Probably." Looking at Sam's sad eyes makes me want to go on talking. "Sam," I say, "there's something I need to tell you. It's about a little boy named Edin."

"Is he a friend of your brother's?"

I hesitate. "You could say that. Edin lived in Bosnia. Last

141

Thursday he was walking through a field with his brother, Mirsad. He was killed by a land mine, and his brother lost one of his legs below the knee." Sam picks at the tape on the handle of his briefcase. His eyes are very dark.

"Mikey doesn't know," I tell him, "and I wasn't supposed to find out. But now that I have ... I don't know what to do with the information."

"You could say a prayer for him," Sam says.

"I wouldn't be the best person to do that. I don't have much experience."

"God understands," Sam says. "I have five prayer times every day. Sometimes I need to do two prayers at once if I get up late, or have a basketball game after school. Sometimes I pray sitting on the bus."

"I thought you had to kneel on the floor to pray," I say. I can't quite see Sam doing that while using public transportation.

"I prostrate myself when I can, but that doesn't always work. Like I said, God is understanding."

"Would you say a prayer for Edin, then? In case I can't get the hang of it?"

"If you ask me to," Sam says, "of course I will." I know he means it, because even though the corners of his mouth turn up, his eyes are still sad.

*A*ll the way to L.A. I imagine there are red flags in the middle of the hallway showing me where it's safe to walk. If I move even ten centimetres off that path, it might be the last step I ever take. When I get to the classroom, Mr. Melnyk sends me on to the office. Danger and red flags again. People in Bosnia have to live this way all the time, but I wasn't expecting it to happen to me.

I don't think there's too much you'd want to know about the meeting Uncle Martin, Mr. Wills, and I have when I get to the office. Uncle Martin starts out a touch macho, I think. He tells Mr. Wills there's obviously a problem in the school and if it isn't cleared up, he's taking me out. He says he can't believe that things are worse at JAWS than at the high school where he teaches art. "We have some difficult students," he says, "but we don't allow this kind of intimidation." He plunks the note down on Mr. Wills's desk.

Mr. Wills hasn't brought out tea and homemade muffins this time, but after he reads the note, he does his best to smooth Uncle Martin's rumples. "I'm aware there's a problem at J. A. Wyndotte School, Mr. Mackelwain," he says. "That's why I was brought in here as principal in the first place. But I can't clear anything up if kids like Nell won't take me into their confidence."

I feel uncomfortable, and twist around in my chair, but Uncle Martin seems to connect with what he's hearing. He starts talking about how he's struggling to give Mikey and me a good home while our mother is away. "Perhaps if Nell had felt she could confide in me earlier ..." he says, like it's a statement.

Now Mr. Wills connects. "It's difficult to be a good parent at the best of times," he says. They both look sympathetically at each other. As it turns out, I don't have to worry about what I want to say, because it's sort of like I'm not there.

"With Nell's mother away on peacekeeping duties in Bosnia ..." Uncle Martin starts out. He leaves this sentence hanging in the air too.

All along Mr. Wills has been polite enough not to ask me where my mother is. I've been hoping he thinks she ran off somewhere, and doesn't want to bring up the subject in case it's too painful for me too speak about. Now he looks at Uncle Martin as though he's just learned that my mother is searching for the Holy Grail.

Mr. Wills, as it turns out, is an old air force man. When I was describing his office earlier, I probably didn't mention that there's this faded picture of a guy standing beside an airplane on the wall by the door. I didn't mention it because the guy in the picture has really big ears and doesn't look like anybody in particular. But I guess it's Mr. Wills a long time ago. What little hair he's got left now is longish and covers over his ears so you don't notice them. But if you really look at them, they're still big. In a way it's good to know that some things about people don't change.

Now that he knows my mother's off trying to keep the peace in Bosnia, Mr. Wills seems even more upset that her daughter, being me, isn't safe in his own school. He tells us what he's going to do about it, like he's swearing allegiance to the Canadian flag.

"Bonnie's coming back today, and I'll send her right back home again. This time she'll be out for a week because of bullying Nell in Mr. Melnyk's room on Halloween. Also, for her involvement in the threatening note. I'll also suspend Shane for three days because of the way he's harassed Nell in her Foods class and in the school halls. And for his part in the note passing. And I'll be talking to their parents, as soon as I can arrange a meeting."

"What if that doesn't work?" I ask. They both turn and look at me like they'd forgotten I was there. "I hear that Bonnie wants to get in as much trouble as she can, so her parents will kick her out. She's telling people her stepmother is really mean."

Mr. Wills gets wrinkles in his forehead. "I'm not sure where you heard that." It isn't exactly a question, so I don't answer. "Bonnie made that claim to me too. I've talked to her father and stepmother and they do admit they're having problems with her at home, but they seem quite concerned about her welfare. Even so," he goes on, with his mouth in a very straight line, "if we have any more problems with Bonnie – if she doesn't maintain her school work and generally keep the peace – I'll expel her from the school permanently." He waves that zero tolerance flag again.

This is a little more like the windowless van I was expecting on the day of the Emily Carr episode, when all the trouble started. But back then, I thought my troubles would be over if Shane disappeared. I didn't even know Bonnie existed. Now I'm not so sure what it will take to get my life back to normal again.

Just before we leave, Mr. Wills invites our family to be special guests at the JAWS Remembrance Day ceremony. The eleventh is actually on Saturday, but schools are doing their remembering on the day before. Uncle Martin apologizes but says he's already taken time off from school this week for today's meeting and can't come. Then Mr. Wills looks at me. "Perhaps you'd like to participate, Nell?" he says.

"Well," I say, "I'm planning on going to Mary Chase for Remembrance Day. I'd like to be with my little brother." I'd geared myself up to tell the truth this morning, and that would have been it – even before Mrs. Montcrieff gave me a special invitation – if I hadn't left out how much I'd hate standing up in front of kids at JAWS. Still, I figure it's a step in the right direction.

*J*AWS doesn't have a specific lunch room, so kids sit on the floor in front of their lockers while a teacher patrols the area to keep everyone quiet and behaving. It doesn't exactly promote digestion. Anyway, I chew my way through a cheese sandwich and an apple, and finish off my apple-cherry juice box. Multiply that by eight and it's most of a week's food supply for that old lady Mom visits, although a little heavy on the fruit and juice.

I go into the library when it opens at 12:15. I figure I'll

just read a magazine, but Sam has signed up the computer next to him for me, and he motions for me to come over. I hadn't been planning to write my mom so soon after I talked to her, but it seems like the opportunity to do that is opening up for me, so that's what I decide to do.

Subject:	**A Real Letter!**
Date:	November 6, 2000
From:	<mmackelwain@hotmail.com>
To:	mail466@dnd.ca

Dear Mom,

This is just to say thanks for calling me. I know I've been pretty awful since you left, but I guess I felt you were more worried about Mikey and about kids in Bosnia than you were about me. I know that's no excuse for being a pill.

Uncle Martin and I had a meeting with the principal today, and he's suspended both the kids who have been harassing me, so that's probably the end of that. Please don't worry.

I really am sorry about Edin. I hope you're not too upset that I know about him. I'm actually not supposed to, but I looked in the letter you sent to Uncle Martin. I realize it was marked PRIVATE, but I thought it was about me and I wanted to know what you were saying. I also realize that sometimes I think everything is about me, when lots of times it isn't. Anyway, please don't tell Uncle Martin I looked. If you do he'll be very upset and he's just barely learning how to handle us as it is. I promise I won't read the PRIVATE stuff any more.

I've made one friend at school. His name is Sam – at least that's what people call him. He thinks what you're doing in Bosnia is great. That could be partly because he's a Muslim, but it's also because he's a Canadian, and a good person. He's blown away that you wear a uniform and carry a gun. His mother stays at home most of the time.

Are you going to write Mikey about what happened? He's so excited about helping Edin. All the kids in his class are. I don't see how we can tell him that someone that young has been killed. It doesn't sound like peace when you think about it.

The bell's about to ring so I have to go now, Mom.

Love,

Nell

PS Maybe I'll stay at JAWS for a bit. (JAWS is my name for this school.) Until I see if things really do get better, at least. I don't think it would be right to make a big stink and then leave. Do you?

Love (again),

Nell (again)

Chapter Seventeen

*I*t's amazing the way Mikey has changed in the last while.
Every day he comes home involved in some new activity.
Last week it was the book collection. Then writing letters to
peacekeepers at Grey Wolf as well as to the kids in the V. K.
school. And collecting school supplies for them. Last Friday
he was on about the peacekeeper who was going to come to
school for Remembrance Day. By Monday he had discov-
ered a good Web site and was working on a power point
presentation for the assembly on the kind of work peacekeepers are doing in Bosnia. The librarian volunteered to
help him and some of the kids in the computer club are
helping him as well.

Today, which is Thursday, he just casually tells me that
one of the kids in his class has a parent who works in the
mayor's office. Since most of the peacekeepers in V. K. right
now are from the Edmonton Battalion, the mayor is going
to visit them in a few weeks. And get this. The mayor would
like to come to Mary Chase on Remembrance Day to present students with a special award for the work they're all

doing. He'd also like to have his picture taken with Mrs. Montcrieff's whole class so he can show it to people at Grey Wolf. I guess Mikey has known this all week, but has been too busy to mention it.

Speaking for myself, the week started out well enough. I actually enjoyed myself in Foods on Tuesday. With Shane away, Sam and Priscilla and I really got along. We made those high-energy food logs for the overnight camp-out. We all had a little taste before we wrapped them up and put them in the freezer. After she finished swallowing, Priscilla started rolling her eyes and reading stuff off the blackboard out loud and really fast. Sam and I broke out laughing.

"Priscilla," Sam said, "what's going on?"

Then she slowed down, like she was unwinding. "I think it's those food logs," she said. "They gave me high energy. Maybe we should give some to the teachers." We all laughed together, like we were kids in Grade Seven.

Wednesday wasn't so great, though. I got to my locker in the morning and found the door standing open. Someone had hung a catnip mouse on my coat hook. I mean, really hung it! By the NECK! It's head was smeared with something sticky and red. I didn't scream, because it obviously wasn't real, but I didn't get a warm, fuzzy feeling, either.

Sam came up while I was standing there. "You didn't get your own lock, did you?" he asked.

I ignored his question and asked my own. "What's that stuff on its head?"

He took the mouse down and sniffed at it. "It's ketchup," he said. "Is this a joke or something?"

I hadn't told Sam about the gift I got through the mail slot the day after Halloween, so I needed to explain. He didn't say much – just went and got his lock, and traded it to me for mine. I promised I'd get my own on the weekend. Sam offered to get rid of the mouse, but I wrapped it up in a couple of Kleenexes and put it in my pocket – I guess to remind myself I wasn't out of trouble yet.

During my lunch hour, I took it to Mr. Wills. "Someone put this in my locker," I said. I dangled it out in front of me. "It's what I get for talking to you."

"You'll have to explain," Mr. Wills said.

I did. I explained that Shane and Bonnie call me "Mouse" when they're not calling me "Smelly" or something worse. I explained that even when they're suspended, their friends aren't. I mentioned the mouse through the mail slot. And I told him how easy it is to get the combination to any lock in the school – unless it's one you've bought yourself. He had smoke coming out of his ears when I'd finished.

I think that's when I finally began to understand something. Mr. Wills can interview all the students he wants to – ask them if they saw anyone around my locker – try to find out who was in the halls during the morning. He can make rules and suspend every fourth student in school, but it's like he said. It won't be worth much, unless kids like me have the courage to cooperate.

What Sam said had been in the back of my mind ever since I talked to him on Monday – I mean about praying for Edin. I still didn't have a clear idea of what to do, but after dinner last night, I got a white candle out of the kitchen, and put it in a candleholder. I took it into my room, put it on the nightstand, and lit it. Then I just sat there, watching the candle flame, waiting for some words to come.

After quite a while they still hadn't, but Mikey had. He opened the door – without knocking, which is his specialty – and wanted to know what I was doing. Like most kids, he's really attracted to candlelight.

"I'm waiting," I said, "and thinking."

"About what?" he wanted to know.

"About how all kids deserve to be safe, no matter where they are."

Mikey went on standing in the doorway for a while. Then he went off somewhere. I was impressed by how quietly he moved away.

It's today I want to talk about, though. Shane's in school again, but Mr. Melnyk has moved him to another group and is letting ours stay just as it is. Shane doesn't look at me or say boo. I don't look at him directly either, but I kind of watch him out of the corner of my eye and I don't see him doing the claw thing even once, to anybody.

Mr. Wills called Uncle Martin yesterday and told him that Shane's parents were very upset about the kind of things he's been saying and doing. He's supposed to be writing me a letter of apology, which I can't wait to see. Also, Ziad told Sam that Shane is grounded for a month. His parents said that if he ever lets Bonnie come near him again, they'll take him out of JAWS and send him to some very strict boy's school out in the country. Mr. Morrison is a hotshot in a bank, and apparently they can afford to do that if they have to.

It's not so easy to say what's happening with Bonnie. Mr. Wills says her parents are trying to get her into some kind of counselling program, but Ziad hasn't heard a word about her. It's almost like she's disappeared, which is okay with me, but I don't think it's exactly fair to make it sound like she's the cause of Shane's obnoxious behaviour. I'm positive he was obnoxious way before he even knew who Bonnie was. Look at the way he acts around the other guys, for example.

That little club at the bottom of the stairs has been broken up, by the way. Tuesday when I went to my locker at noon, Mr. Wills was standing there pretty much by himself. I guess rating girls and embarrassing them as they walk by isn't much fun when the principal is listening. Especially one who means what he says and does what he says he'll do.

I realize I'm changing my tune a little about Mr. Wills, but don't they say that it's a woman's prerogative to change her mind? So what if I'm not a woman yet? I'm definitely edging up on it.

I've been eating lunch at JAWS all week, and then going into the library afterwards. Uncle Martin agrees we have to let things die down before I can come and go pretty much like I did before. Bonnie's still in the world somewhere, after all, and we're not sure what she'll do next.

Today, Sam comes over to my locker about halfway through lunch and sits with me. He has pita bread and some pasty stuff called hummus that's loaded with garlic. "My mother gave me too much," he says. "Would you like some?" It feels a little bit like having lunch with Uncle Martin, but I don't want to hurt Sam's feelings, so I try it.

After I get past the garlic, which has quite a kick to it, I decide I can live with this hummus stuff, even if it does sound sort of like what you call leaves decomposing on the forest floor.

"Here," I say, "want to try some of my chocolate chip cookies?"

I know they're not exotic. We've even made them in Foods before, but Sam says, "Sure," and bites into one. "It's good," he says. Crumbs fall down on his T-shirt and he flicks them off. "Did you make them?" I give a little happy-homemaker nod.

"Some day you can try my mother's baklava." He tells me it's a dessert with walnuts and honey and ground-up pistachios all wrapped up in a papery crust.

"Great." It sounds like we're candidates for the Highlands Senior Citizen Centre. We'll probably be trading recipes and sharing headache remedies before long.

"I've got something else for you," Sam says. He hands me a twist of orange tissue paper. "It's from my sister, Maryam. I've told her about your mother. And about you. And Edin. She works in a gift shop and she wants you to have this."

I untwist the paper. Inside is a little mirror in a flower-shaped frame of pink plastic. It has a magnet on the back. "I don't know what to say," I tell him. And I don't. I'm not big on looking at myself in mirrors, but it's an amazing thing for her to do.

"It sticks on your locker," Sam says. "Maryam says girls like to check their makeup and things before they go to class." Maybe that's when he notices for the first time that I don't wear any makeup.

"It's really nice of her," I say, not wanting him to be embarrassed.

All week I've been wondering about Sam's other name – the one Ziad called him when he came to the house – but there hasn't been a good time to ask him about it. Now, as he folds up his red nylon lunch bag and gets to his feet,

I decide to. Sam hesitates for a minute, then sits back down again. "My name is Methael," he says. "It's a great honour, because Methael is the name of an angel."

"Then how come you don't want people to call you that?" I ask.

"It's not that I don't want them to," he tells me, "but Canadians usually pronounce it wrong. When I first went to school, kids called me "Metal" or "Metal Head." Some days I came home crying. Samaer is my second name, so my parents agree that I can be called that. Sam is my idea."

He stands up again, walks over to the recycle can, and tosses in his juice box. I follow behind him, and we both turn toward the stairs. "Your mother didn't like it when I called you that, though," I say.

"My parents don't acknowledge the name. And they didn't like it that you called me at all. I thought I explained about that."

"Would they like it that we sometimes hang around together at school?"

"They already know. I've told them that your mother is a peacekeeper in Bosnia and that you need a friend."

I'm not sure what kind of answer I was expecting from Sam, but that wasn't it. Suddenly I feel like I'm some kind of charity case, so I say, "Don't put yourself out on my account. I haven't had a friend for a long time, and I've survived." Then I speed into the library without him. I don't go to the computers, though. I sit in the corner by myself and read a magazine.

I know. It's an immature thing to do. But I'm kind of edgy today, and sitting in the corner by myself is probably a good idea right now, no matter how I got here. It gives me time to think, and I need to do that.

All week long it's like I've been waiting for something bad to happen. "Waiting for the other shoe to drop," I think people call it, although I have no idea where the expression comes from. It's possible the person who made it up lived in the basement of a boarding house – maybe even the one Emily Carr owned. Someone in the room above probably came in late at night, sat on the bed, and dropped one of his shoes on the bare wood floor. Then nothing – whoever it was in the basement stayed awake all night waiting for the other one to fall. When he went to work the next day, he was tired and bleary-eyed. A co-worker asked, "Rough night?"

"Yes," he answered. "The guy above me in the boarding house dropped a shoe on the floor about two a.m. and woke me up. He works construction, and from the sound of it, each one weighs fifty pounds. I kept waiting for him to drop the other one, but he didn't, and I never got back to sleep."

Of course, it could be a woman who comes in late and drops her shoe. She'd probably be wearing sandals or shoes with high heels, though, and they wouldn't make much noise. Even so, why doesn't she drop the other shoe on the floor right away? Does she fall asleep and keep it on all night?

I suppose she might only have one shoe on in the first place. Maybe she has a sore foot and is wearing a sock or slipper on it. The person below could wait forever and never hear THAT hit the floor.

Or maybe she only has one shoe to drop because she only has one foot. Maybe she's lost the other one the way the little boy in Bosnia did. Mirsad, I mean. The one who survived. My thoughts still keep going back to that.

*I*t's possible, of course, that everything I've just been thinking is a way of avoiding what's really wiggling around in my mind somewhere. And that's this. How come Sam is proud to have a name that most people can't even pronounce – while I have a name that's very easy to say, and I hate it?

Almost everyone likes angels, of course. They're powerful figures. But Nellie McClung wasn't exactly a wimp. She lived at the beginning of the twentieth century, when Canadian women weren't considered people, and couldn't vote or own property. She and some other women went to court to prove that they WERE people. That sounds like power to me.

"Nellie Hopkins," I say under my breath. If people notice me talking to myself, I'm not even aware of it. "Nellie Hopkins." I'm not crazy about the way it sounds, and I'm not thrilled that it rhymes with words like Smelly. But hey! I'm not responsible for other people's bad poetry.

Nellie Hopkins. Maybe I can grow into it. I hear the name in my head all the way to my Social Studies class, and I swear I'm a little taller by the time I get there.

At the end of the day, I figure it's my turn to go to Sam's locker. I apologize and remind him that I won't be at school tomorrow morning because of the Remembrance Day Ceremony at Mary Chase. And I give him a note for his sister. It just says, "Thank you for thinking of me, Nellie Hopkins." But it's in my best calligraphy, and it looks good. ALL of it.

"I'm going out the front door today," I tell Sam. "Shane is leaving me alone. Bonnie's laying low. I need things to get back to normal. I think it will be all right."

I hardly give a thought to red flags or land mines as I walk over to pick up my brother.

I can understand why those little boys went off into an unmarked part of some farmer's field. They probably heard a strange noise. Or thought they saw something shining in the trees and wanted to find out what it was.

Sometimes you just get tired of watching where you put your feet.

Chapter Eighteen

*T*he Remembrance Day assembly at Mary Chase is pretty impressive. I'm not just saying that because my little brother has had a lot to do with it. Or because he's waiting for me when I come into the school and absolutely woofing with pride when he sees me. I think anybody would be impressed with the kind of ceremony the school has organized.

For starters, Mayor J. J. Jones is sitting at the front of the gym, along with the principal, Mrs. Harris, and a couple of people I've never seen before. There are several television cameras in the room, because of the mayor, I suppose. In fact, the only reason I recognize him is because I've seen him so many times on the six o'clock news.

There are about twenty chairs at the back for visitors. Mrs. Montcrieff even lets me sit on one. "I'm so pleased you've arranged to be with us today, Nell," she says, like she hasn't improved my life by letting me come.

As the teachers bring their classes into the gym, I start to feel this hum of energy. By the time the gym is ready to lift off the ground and go into orbit over the river valley, a guy in long socks and a kilt comes in playing the bagpipes. Suddenly it's quiet, and I get goosebumps that don't go completely away.

The piper is followed by a colour party that marches in with the Canadian flag in front, and the Alberta and United Nations flags behind. After them, the peacekeeper comes in wearing his everyday military gear. He tells us later that he'd normally wear a dress uniform, but he got permission to wear his working clothes so we can see how Lester B. Hopkins's mother dresses when she's on the job. He asks us to stand and sing "Oh Canada," which we do. The kids don't mumble the words, either. They stand up straight and sing from their toes. So do most of the rest of us.

Everything goes along very smoothly after that. Mikey's power point presentation is good, considering a little kid in Grade Two did most of it. He's downloaded pictures of Camp Grey Wolf and the village of V.K. And he has a picture of one of the de-mining teams working with Sherlock and Watson. At least that's who he likes to think the dogs in the picture are.

Mrs. Harris doesn't talk for long and I'm glad, because little kids can easily start to fidget. The mayor also keeps it short. Mostly he presents Mrs. Montcrieff with an Edmonton Good Citizen Certificate for all the work her class has done. She asks them all to stand, because they're the ones who deserve recognition. Then she asks Mikey to stand and says he got the whole thing started. After that she asks me to stand as well, so that people can see both the amazing children of the equally amazing Master Corporal Alice S. Mackelwain. I don't feel too self-conscious, because they're mostly little kids in the room. And I don't even mind that everyone is calling my mother by her military title. I know there are people who need her as much as I do. I guess it won't kill me to share her.

*R*ight at eleven o'clock we have a moment's silence. It's so quiet in the room you can tell that some people have colds and should be home in bed. Then the peacekeeper gets up to talk.

His name is Andrew MacDonald and he says he's originally from Prince Edward Island. I think he has a few notes in front of him, but he mostly just speaks from his head. He tells us he was in Bosnia four years ago, when things were still very unsettled. He admits it was hard to be there then. He says a few people saw things that were so disturbing they couldn't forget them. He doesn't say what they saw and I'm glad about that.

"Speaking for myself," he goes on, "I'm proud that I was able to help get things back to normal. It was hard work. We had to be out there, making our presence felt all the time, but in the end, I think people breathed easier because we were there."

Then he makes a little joke that goes over very well. He says Mrs. Montcrieff wants him to talk to us about peace –

what it is and how you keep it. "That's a pretty tough question," he says. "If your teacher makes you answer questions like that every day, you're all probably geniuses at this school. Or you soon will be." Mikey and the other kids in Mrs. Montcrieff's classroom cheer for her. Other kids in the school join in.

I'm hoping he isn't going to duck the whole thing and say how peace is different for each person and we all have to answer that question for ourselves. I'm really tired of questions with answers that don't really tell you anything. And I'm pleased that he actually tries to do what Mrs. Montcrieff asked him to.

"All I can say," he tells us, "is that peace isn't everybody liking each other and getting along all the time. Peace is what you do when that doesn't happen. How you work together to make sure that people who aren't getting along are still treated fairly. How you try to help them learn to get along, even when it looks like they can't." Then he thanks us and the reverse of everything that opened the assembly happens and it all closes down again. The music and the flag and the sound of marching and orders all go back to some quiet place, waiting, I guess, until we need them to come out again.

When people get up and begin to leave, Mrs. Montcrieff motions for me to come over. Then she introduces Mikey and me to the mayor and we get our pictures taken with him. I feel a little self-conscious, but Mikey flashes one of his great smiles and doesn't bark or do anything remotely embarrassing. Then the mayor leaves. It takes me some time to convince my little brother that we still have to eat whether we're going to be on the six o'clock news or not. Eventually we leave the school, though. Uncle Martin asked me this morning if I was ready to try coming home at noon and I said, "Yes. It looks like it's pretty safe. What can happen?"

*I*f you want my advice, you'll avoid sending questions like that out into the universe, because they may come back to you in ways you're not ready for. Mikey and I are a block away from Mary Chase and about two blocks from home. Most of the kids are already off the streets and eating lunch because it's taken us a little while to get going. Then I hear whistling and yelling. I turn around and see Bonnie about a block behind us with two other girls. I'm sure it's Bonnie, even though what I can actually see at that distance is three black silhouettes. As soon as I stop and turn around to look at them, they begin to run in our direction.

I guess there was another shoe, after all.

*I*f I was alone I could probably outrun Bonnie and company. She's a smoker – I'm not. And you know how much confidence I have in my legs. But I'm not alone. I've got Mikey with me, and he couldn't keep up. Standing there, all I can think about is that he's had a great day and she shouldn't be allowed to ruin it. Really. I'm not trying to sound like a martyr or anything, but that's what's going through my head.

"Mikey," I say. "Go on home. Get the spare key from in back of the house and go inside."

Mikey's eyes are wide open and he looks instantly scared, but he says, "No! I ain't leaving you here." It's a good time for him to try an ungrammatical expression like that, because I can't pay attention to it right now.

"Mikey," I say again. "Get going! I just want to talk to these kids. And you're too little to hear what I'm going to say." Mikey still stands there, shaking his head back and forth. We're facing each other, but I'm turned in the direction Bonnie's coming from and I notice that she's not all that far away now.

I take Mikey by the shoulders, turn him around, and give him a little push. "Lester B. Hopkins," I yell, "move out! That's an order!" I don't know where these words come from, but instead of having a fit like he usually does when I use his real name, he immediately starts to run.

As soon as he does that, I turn around and walk slowly toward Bonnie and her buddies. When we're pretty close together, I call out, "What do you want?" I brace my legs apart and try to look stern. At first it seems like what Bonnie wants is to call me every four- or five-letter word she's ever heard before. There are several she uses more than once. I get the definite impression she hates me and thinks I'm a loser.

I don't answer her back, though. I just keep standing there, trying to make my face neutral. I'm scared and my nerves are kind of frozen, so it isn't too hard. At first, Bonnie's words go past me. Obviously I'm not thrilled to hear the stuff coming out of her mouth, but I don't feel like a loser anymore, so it kind of feels like she's talking about someone else.

Eventually Bonnie runs out of names to call me, and switches to a new track. "I warned you not to talk to anyone," she says, moving closer to me as she talks. "But you didn't listen. Thanks to you," she spits at me, "I can't see Shane any more!" She shoves me in the right shoulder. "Thanks to you, my dad's kicking me out!" She shoves me in the left shoulder, I guess because she doesn't want to show favouritism. "But you wouldn't know what that feels like, since you don't have a father, would you?"

That gets under my skin, but it also confuses me. I thought she WANTED to go to a foster home. Now I don't know what to think.

"I have a dad," I say. "I just don't know where he is." I turn and start to walk away. For a second, I think I'll be able to get away with it, but she comes after me, grabs my arm, and yanks me around. She switches back to name-calling, and then shoves me really hard in the chest. I go backward into an *Edmonton Journal* box.

The other day when she pushed me I managed to keep my balance. This time I don't. I'm pretty upset with myself for going down like a duck in hunting season, and I try to get back up, but I must have twisted my ankle underneath me when I fell. It hurts like you-know-what when I try to put weight on it, so all I can do is sit there and scowl at her.

Bonnie kneels down beside me and sticks her face right into mine. "You think you're so smart," she says, "with your weirdo uncle always nosing into things. And your weirdo mother marching around in army boots."

"You leave my family out of this!" I say.

"I've heard your mother isn't in the army at all," Bonnie smirks. "I've heard she walked out on you, because you're so pathetic. That's why you don't have a real family."

"My mother cares about me," I say back. "And my family is real enough that they put up with me, and they're not kicking me out. That's more than you can say!" Maybe that does set her off, but I'm not about to let her insult my family while I just sit there, attracting flies.

She goes ballistic after that, of course. I think the girls who come with her try to calm her down. "Chill out, Bonnie!" someone says. "Let's go now!" Stuff like that. But whatever they're saying, it doesn't work.

Bonnie grabs my hair and yanks my head back to the ground. Then she punches me in the face. Maybe I start to cry a little then, but not very much. Anyway, who wouldn't?

I do remember girls' voices again. "Chill out, Bonnie! Someone's coming! Let's get out of here." Then there's this sharp pain in my ribs and it's possible I conk out for a minute. The next thing I know for sure, is that I hear what sounds like Mikey's voice, kind of high and far away, calling, "Nellie! Nellie!" I raise myself up on one elbow and see him racing back toward me.

"You're going the wrong way!" I yell at him. "Go home!" After that I lie back down on the ground and listen. My ears have to work very hard at keeping in touch with what's going on, though, because the rest of me is having a time out.

Then Mikey's beside me. His voice is lower than it used to be when he asks, "Are you all right, miss?" A uniform with a guy in it bends over and peers into my face.

"Are we in Bosnia?" I ask.

"This is Edmonton," the voice says.

Then my brother's old voice pipes up. "Why's she talking like that?" he asks. "Why does she want to know if this is Bosnia?"

The low voice says something about concussion and getting an ambulance.

I open the eye that I can still see out of. "If this isn't Bosnia and you're not my brother," I ask the uniform, "why are you dressed like a peacekeeper?" I've just been beaten up, so you can't really blame me for being a little out of it.

Now Mikey leans down next to me. I'm positive it's Mikey, because he says so. "It's your brother," he says. He presses his mouth to my ear, so he's a little on the loud side, but he speaks slowly and distinctly. "He's not a peace-keep-er," he says. "He's not in the arm-y. He's a se-cur-ity guard. I went to the block par-ent house on the cor-ner and he was there."

"Oh," I say. I'm tired. I decide to have a little rest. I'm pretty sure I deserve it.

Chapter Nineteen

I know reality's important, but sometimes I DO wish life could be more like it is in the movies. You know how some of them end, with the future of all the people who are in it flashing on the screen? I'd love it if that kind of information could appear in front of my eyes right now. I can just about see the words scrolling over my bed with decorated letters at the beginning of each new section.

Recently, Nell Hopkins bought an island in the Caribbean where she lives in seclusion, leaving its shores only to attend frequent reunions with her family. (Most of her family, that is. The whereabouts of her father, Robert Hopkins, are still unknown.) Miss Hopkins's book, How to Survive on a Desert Island, *has topped the* New York Times *Best-Seller List for the past twenty-five weeks.*

Lester B. Hopkins lives in Edmonton but commutes to Toronto where he is director of the Canadian Save the Children Foundation.

Alice S. Mackelwain divides her time between New York, where she is Canada's representative to the United Nations, and

Edmonton, where she, her brother, Martin Mackelwain, and his wife, Christine Stuart, operate an art gallery, theatre, and shelter for homeless children.

Bonnie Lewis and Shane Morrison (a.k.a. Claws Mireau) recently held up a bank in Calgary, Alberta, and at this moment are still at large.

Unfortunately, life doesn't work that way. In the real world, when the future gets here, it's called the present. Already, I have to start thinking about mine.

"I don't want to rush you, Nell," Uncle Martin said to me yesterday. That was Tuesday, November 14, by the way, and not an unlucky day on any calendar I've ever heard of. "But it's been four days since you and Bonnie had your altercation. We at least need to start talking about your school situation. It will be better for all of us when things get back to normal." I interpret that to mean that he DOES want to rush me, and has every intention of doing so.

But who am I to talk? Maybe I'm rushing you. Maybe you're curious about what I've been doing since I got my lights punched out on November 10. I'm not really clear about a lot of it. For instance, I don't remember getting to the hospital, although Mikey says the security guy took me in his car. (He's the one I understandably thought was a peacekeeper.)

I do know that Uncle Martin picked me up and drove me home. It seemed like we were going about twenty kilometres an hour, and he kept saying, "Are you all right, Nell? Are you okay?" over and over like a broken record.

I guess I did look pretty banged up. I had scratches all over my face, my left eye was swollen shut, and my ankle was wrapped up like it belonged to an Egyptian mummy. I also had a very big bruise on my ribs where Bonnie kicked me. That part didn't show, but it made me dislike breathing, so I moaned and winced a lot.

When we got home I went right to bed. Uncle Martin gave me ice in zip-lock baggies and Mikey, who'd been I don't know where all this time, ran back and forth to get new ice from the refrigerator and keep me absolutely freezing. Thanks to the shock of the whole incident and also to the little football-shaped painkillers Uncle Martin picked up at the drug store on the way home, I didn't feel cold too long, though. I fell asleep almost right away.

I hardly remember anything about the twenty-four hours after that. Uncle Martin says two police officers came to the house Friday evening. They talked to him, and looked in on me while I was out of it and in bed. Later they took a statement from the security guard, who saw Bonnie and her friends running away.

A couple of days later they came back and got a statement from me. One of them told me I was right to send Mikey away. Actually, what he said was, "You did a brave thing, Nell."

*I*t seems like I heard Uncle Martin on the phone a lot at first. I don't have any idea who he was talking to, although I am positive it wasn't my mother. When we were coming home from the hospital, I made him promise he wouldn't try to make an emergency call to her and freak her out. I figured she'd had enough trouble in the last little while because of me – also because of that awful business with Edin and Mirsad. I didn't want to make her cry again.

*I*do remember that Mr. Wills came to visit me Saturday evening. He brought me a red rose, wrapped up inside a clear plastic tube. I always thought red roses were for love, but he told me they can also be for courage. That isn't the kind of thing I'd expect him to know, so I'll bet Mrs. Wills checked it out for him on the Internet. Mr. Wills told me how sorry he was about what happened. He said they needed me at the school and that he and Mr. Melnyk really wanted me to come back.

It's kind of funny when you think about it. A month ago if I'd thought I had the slightest chance to leave JAWS and go just about anywhere else in Edmonton, I would have been too excited to sleep for nights on end. But by Monday, when I'd eased off on the painkillers and started to feel like I might be part of the same world as everybody else again, I wasn't sure I had the energy to start all over somewhere else.

Yesterday was an amazing day, though, and I'm clear as glass about that. Mikey came home around four o'clock with Mrs. Montcrieff. She brought me a blue vase full of flowers she'd picked from her garden in the summer and then dried. Mikey was carrying a couple of dozen little cards his classmates had made for me, with flowers and trees and birds and happy little kid suns painted on them. Most of the cards had, "Get Well, Nell," on them, although one little boy decided to be original, if that's a decision you make and not something you just can't help. He wrote, "Good Will, Nell," on his. I smiled at that. Then Mikey noticed, and he started laughing. That got Mrs. Montcrieff going. I wanted to join in, but my ribs are still tender, so I gritted my teeth and breathed out my nose like a bull at the rodeo until the urge passed.

Just as Mrs. Montcrieff was going out the front door, Christine came up the sidewalk. She had a long rehearsal break, so she'd brought me some chocolate fudge she'd made herself. She acted very concerned and sympathetic, which I liked almost more than the candy.

Uncle Martin got home while she was still here. He seemed pleased to see her, but I watched carefully and I didn't see a lot of colour change in his face. I guess I was on the wrong track about their relationship. In fact it makes sense for her to be like a sister to him instead of a girlfriend. She's older and kind of mature, so since he hasn't been able to talk to my mom about how her children are driving him crazy, I guess he's been talking to Christine instead.

The big surprise, though – the main event, really – was Tuesday evening. I couldn't have predicted this with a thousand-watt crystal ball. It was so amazing that I want to lay it out for you, just like it happened.

Mikey and Uncle Martin and I are all sitting on the floor in the living room playing Monopoly. That way we can all be on the same level, and the blood doesn't rush to my ankle. Uncle Martin owns about half the board and is really cleaning up, so Mikey's attention is beginning to wander. He lies down and just accidentally cleans the hotels off Park Avenue with his elbow. Uncle Martin tells him to be careful and puts the hotels back in place. It's obviously time to let the game go, but he doesn't see it that way. Like I've said before, he still has things to learn.

Mikey crawls over toward the TV. He picks up the remote control and holds it politely, waiting for Uncle Martin to get the message. Then he must hear something, because he stands up, goes to the window, and pokes his head out the opening in the curtains. When he pulls his head back out again, he says, "Did you call a taxi, Uncle Martin?"

"I haven't called a taxi in fifteen years, Mike," Uncle Martin says. "Why would I do that?" He's about to collect the last few dollars in my bank account because I've landed on Marvin Gardens where he has a house AND a hotel.

"I'm bankrupt," I say. "I'm out."

"I could arrange financing for you," Uncle Martin says. I'm ready to accuse him of being a loan shark when the doorbell rings. Uncle Martin looks up from the pile of hundred-dollar bills he's attempting to pass on to me at what he imagines to be a modest rate of interest.

"It's the taxi," Mikey says.

"Just in time, too," I chime in. "You can get to the airport and out of town before the police find out you're making money off of minors."

Uncle Martin gets up, walks to the door, and opens it. There, standing on the front porch, is Sam. "Hello, sir," he says.

"Hello," Uncle Martin says back. "May I help you?"

"I just came to see Nell," Sam says.

"Nell?" Uncle Martin asks, like the name is vaguely familiar to him but he can't quite connect it with a face.

"Yes, sir," Sam says. "Your niece."

"You came in a cab?" Uncle Martin asks, still a few beats behind.

"My father," Sam says. "He'll wait for me." Uncle Martin opens the door and Sam walks into the house.

Chapter Twenty

All the time Sam and Uncle Martin have been talking, I've been sitting on the floor like I'm back on medication again, wishing I wasn't wearing the rattiest sweatsuit I own. The knees and seat bag out and there's a hole in at least one of the elbows. I fluff up my hair with my fingers as he comes in the door. "Hello, Sam," I say.

Uncle Martin motions for Sam to sit down. Sam hands him a paper plate with tinfoil pressed down over the top. "It's baklava," he says. "From my mother to your family."

"Baklava," Uncle Martin says, suddenly back on track. "That's with walnuts and honey and cinnamon?"

"In my family we put ground pistachios in it too," Sam says. "Also another secret ingredient. My mother got the recipe from her mother."

Sam sits down on the couch. I stay on the floor, Mikey plunks down right next to me, and Uncle Martin takes the chair opposite us and beside the window. We all look at Sam.

"Everyone's heard about what happened to Nell," he

says. "And we're very sorry." Even though he's talking about me, he's mostly looking at Uncle Martin. I'm learning that's a male thing, but I'm a little disappointed that Sam's falling into it so automatically. "My brother Ziad wants me to give you his apology," he says.

"It's not Ziad's fault," I say.

Sam looks directly at me now. "But he said he would watch out for you."

I look at Uncle Martin, hoping to cue him in. Amazingly, it works. "Of course it isn't your brother's fault," he says. "We don't hold him responsible in any way." Then he stands up. "Would you like something to drink?" He lists what we've got – orange juice, ginger ale, and lemonade.

"No thank you, sir," Sam says. "But please have some baklava if you're hungry."

Uncle Martin goes into the kitchen to put the dessert on a plate. Or maybe to give us some privacy. I suppose that's also remotely possible. Mikey's still sticking to me, though, ever vigilant and on the job.

"Your eye looks sore," Sam says.

Mikey pipes up. "You should see her ribs! They used to be dark blue and then green. But now they're going yellow."

"Mike!" I say.

Sam smiles. "You must be Nell's brother," he says.

Mikey smiles back. It's the old wide-gap special again, and it's just as bright as ever. "I'm Lester B. Hopkins," he says. The list of people who can call him that is really growing.

"My eye doesn't bother me," I say, "and my ankle is a bit

better, although I still have to keep it wrapped. My ribs are still sore, though, so don't try to make me laugh."

"I won't," Sam says.

"Your father doesn't mind that you're here?" I ask.

"I had things to bring you," he says. "I know Mr. Wills sent your books home already, but I needed my lock back, and I didn't want to leave this in your locker." He hands me the mirror Maryam gave me.

I look in it and examine the neon ring around my eye. "I'm still here," I say. "I haven't disappeared or anything. I guess that's a good use for a mirror."

Sam takes a yellow envelope out of his pocket and holds it out to me. "A lot of other people want you to know they're thinking about you."

I open the envelope. There's a card inside with a stone gargoyle on the front. He's sticking his tongue out and looking sad or mad or sick to his stomach. It's hard to tell which. On the inside of the card it says,

"Open your mouth and say you're coming back soon."

People have written all over the card. Mr. Melnyk says, "Prosperity Makes Friends, Adversity Tries Them." It's by Publilius Syrus, whoever he might be. Underneath that Mr. Melnyk adds, "Don't give up on us, Nell. Bill Melnyk." For some reason I've never thought about Mr. Melnyk having a first name like Bill. Actually, I've never thought of him having a first name at all.

Mr. Wills has one too. It's Nelson. He writes, "Best wishes for your speedy recovery, Nelson S. Wills." His words are kind of like the flower he brought, all sealed up tight. But I appreciate the fact that he wrote something.

Lots of kids have written to me. Priscilla Wong says, "Come back to Foods! We don't have any energy without you." Others from that class have added their names. Most of them I've never talked to. One girl named Anna Balsam says, "Thanks for getting this class cleaned up." And a guy named Ray says, "Girls Named Nell Rule!" and underlines it. Shane's name isn't on the card. My teeth would fall out if it was.

"It's mostly kids from Foods who signed," Sam says. "Except for Karen Lavoie." He points to her name. "She caught me in the hall and asked if she could put her name on the card." What she writes is, "Maybe I was wrong about the matches. I'm not sure we'll ever get a fire started without you." I smile.

"Is this from your brother?" I ask. I point to a big red Z at the bottom of the card. There are two eyes on top it, and a long nose that hangs over the edge.

Sam smiles and shrugs. "Who else?"

"This is pretty incredible," I say. After that I don't know where to go with the conversation. But Sam does.

"We hear you're not coming back."

"She hasn't made up her mind," Mikey blurts out. I give him a sharp look.

"I'm thinking about it." Now Mikey nods like that's what he meant in the first place.

"Well," Sam says, "we'd really like it if you would."

Uncle Martin comes back into the living room with the baklava on a pink glass plate and four glasses of lemonade on a tray. "Yum," Mikey says. He takes one of the glasses before Uncle Martin can set the tray down on the coffee table.

"Mike," Uncle Martin says. "Guests first."

Sam stands up. "It's okay," he says, "I have to go. My father will need to get back to work."

Uncle Martin can't send him off with anything. Sam brought the baklava as a gift, after all, and people don't march off into the night carrying glasses of lemonade. So he thanks Sam for coming and walks to the door with him. I get up off the floor because I think it's important, and limp along behind with Mikey.

All three of us stand at the door watching Sam as he walks out to the taxi, opens the door, gets in, and closes it again. Just as Sam's father drives away, he flashes his head-lights three times.

"Why did he do that?" Mikey wants to know.

"It's like a ten-gun salute," I say, "only shorter."

"That's one way of putting it," Uncle Martin says. He closes the door.

We sit around for a while sipping lemonade and eating baklava. Mikey declares he really likes it. Uncle Martin says the combination of walnuts and pistachios is really interesting. Then he begins to ponder what the secret ingredient might be. Cardamom? Saffron? Mace? He takes another bite and appears to give himself over completely to solving the mystery.

Mikey says to me, "I like Sam. Is he your boyfriend?"

"No," I tell him. "We're friends. Like Uncle Martin and Christine are."

Uncle Martin glances over at us when I say that, and swallows really loudly.

"I thought Christine WAS your girlfriend," Mikey says to Uncle Martin. "Isn't she?"

"Of course we're friends," Uncle Martin says, and then suddenly seems in a great rush to pick up the Monopoly bits from the floor. He's acting pretty fishy. Maybe he's got something going with Christine, after all. I try to pretend I'm her and take a good look at him. He has a little bald spot at the very back of his head that I've never noticed before. He's wearing sandals without socks, and his toes are very long and white. I snort. Christine couldn't possibly be interested in him.

Then it occurs to me that he might have a crush on her, even if she doesn't return it. Uncle Martin is hopeless and all that, but I can't stand to think of him moping around the house, playing death scenes from his favourite operas. I decide to talk to Christine and ask her to let him down gently. Or maybe I should e-mail Mom and get her to talk to Uncle Martin.

After the money is all counted and the houses and hotels and playing pieces are stowed away, I say, "I suppose I could give it another few weeks. Maybe a month."

"You need to be in school before that, Nell," Uncle Martin says. "If you want to find a new one, I'll help as much as I can. But the longer you wait, the harder it will be."

"I mean I could go back to JAWS. J.A. Wyndotte School. Maybe I could try it until Christmas, and see what happens."

"Is that what you want to do?" Uncle Martin asks.

"Yes, Nell," my brother says, like he's Uncle Martin's personal echo, "is that what you want?"

"I didn't say it's what I WANT to do," I snap. "I said I suppose I could give it a TRY. For a while."

Neither of them say anything else. Mikey takes the last piece of baklava and starts to put it in his mouth. Uncle Martin scowls at him, so he puts it back on the plate, picks up the fourth glass of lemonade, and drinks some of it instead.

"That's if nobody objects," I say. Mikey and Uncle Martin shake their heads, but they keep quiet.

I go into the bathroom, get some shampoo and bubble bath, and pick out the biggest towel I can find. It's dark green and feels about as thick as the living-room rug. "I'll need to stay for lunch at first." Still no word from them. I put the plug in the bathtub and turn on the hot water. After a few minutes, clouds of steam start to swirl up and make beads of moisture on the tile walls. "And I'm just trying it out! I'm not making any promises!" I call out one last time. Then I close the door.

Chapter Twenty-One

I'm standing in my L.A. classroom, looking at the wall displays people made to finish up the unit on desert island survival. It's the last day of November, and I've been back in school a little over a week. The lunch bell will go any minute.

They had a vote on what to take while I was away and matches didn't make the list. I'm not upset about it. In the end they actually had some good reasons for eliminating them. One was that matches will only be good until we run out of them, so it's better to know how to make fire from the very beginning. I never mentioned not trusting Ben to anyone, but the idea still came up that we should all sign some kind of agreement to share our skills with each other. That sounds okay to me. I've finally figured out that working with other people can get things done.

Look at what's happened here at JAWS, for instance. I'm not saying it's a prize-winning school all of a sudden, or that the teachers are suddenly full of steam. There's still no choir and classes are about as boring as ever. But things ARE happening. Before I came back to school, Mr. Wills started bringing in people who have experience with bullying to lead weekly discussion groups on the topic in our home-rooms. Sam says that at first the kids didn't say much, but by now they're starting to open up a little. And I certainly have a lot to say. Keeping quiet doesn't get you anywhere in the end – I've got the bruises to prove it.

Speaking of bruises, mine got me a lot more attention than I wanted when I first came back to school. I was still a little colourful, of course – my left eye, especially, wasn't normal, even with the skin-tone makeup Christine gave me to wear. I was also taking it easy on my bad ankle, so I couldn't walk very fast. I kept telling myself people weren't looking at me because I was weird. It was more like they were thinking, "That's the kid Bonnie went after? Her? She's the one all the fuss is about?"

Naturally, there were all kinds of rumours going around. I guess a few still are. It wouldn't be a junior high if that didn't happen. The way some people tell it, Bonnie had three or four kids with her and they all gave me a going over. Others can't believe my little brother and a security guard could scare her away, and figure the police must have pulled her off me. Sam says he's also heard a version where I stand up to Bonnie. Considering the amount of time I spent lying on the ground, that sounds like an odd thing to say. But who am I to argue?

Anyway, I was trying to tell you how JAWS has changed. For one thing, Mr. Wills and Mr. Melnyk and some of the other teachers are out in the halls a lot. They talk to kids and try to keep up with how they're doing. I realize that's something I've missed about living in Beaumont. I'd go to the corner store and the owner would always say, "Nell! How are you! And how's that little brother of yours?"

"He's driving me crazy," I'd say and roll my eyes like I was dying. Then he'd laugh and I'd laugh and buy a pop or something. It was no big deal, but I felt ... I don't know ... like I was in the right place or something. I guess JAWS could be like Beaumont – like a community, I mean. IF people work at it.

That's what makes it so hard to know whether I should change schools. Because of everything that's happened, the academic program I mentioned is making room for me, and I could go there in January. It might be a good idea, but ... let's say I DO make the move. It'll definitely be more interesting, and some of the kids will be okay. People like Shane or Bonnie can STILL be around, though, so that makes it like coming to JAWS all over again, minus the friends I've made here to support me.

I know. I can make NEW friends. I'm getting better at it, and I imagine I will. I guess the thing that's really bothering me is this: how do you leave behind people you care about? Especially after they've put themselves on the line for you?

When the bell rings, I go to my locker and then start down the front stairs. I'm picking Mikey up for lunch today. He likes getting away from school at noon, and walking home and back helps clear my head. These days, I really do have a lot to think about.

I read somewhere that as long as you hate somebody – or they hate you – you have a relationship with them. That, of course, makes me think about Bonnie, who I've been putting off mentioning. I don't want a relationship of any kind with her, so I'm trying to do what I can to eliminate bad feelings on my end. I'm not having much success, though.

Maybe it should help that she's disappeared, but it doesn't seem to. Her parents haven't seen her since Remembrance Day, and I hear they're worried sick – especially her dad. The police are looking for her, but so far they haven't had any luck. They think she's hiding out somewhere in Edmonton. When they do find her, they'll definitely charge her, so I don't imagine she's all that eager to be found.

I told Sam about lighting a candle for Edin. He suggested I do the same thing for Bonnie. "For all we know," he said, "she could be dead."

At first, what he said shocked me. "Edin was an innocent little kid," I told him. "Bonnie's practically a terrorist."

Sam just looked at me. "We don't know everything," is all he said back.

Actually, what Sam said about the candle was, "You

COULD light a candle for Bonnie." He doesn't ever get preachy, although he is very much into spiritual matters right now. Ramadan has just started, and he fasts until sundown every day. Even in Foods, where we've started our Christmas baking unit, Sam never eats anything. Last class we made shortbread, with real butter. He kept taking deep breaths, and saying, "Mmm! That really smells good!" He looked kind of green when we took it out of the oven, but he didn't snitch the tiniest crumb.

"You should get excused from class for the next few weeks," Priscilla told him. "You could do a report in the library instead. It never smells very good in there."

Sam didn't think it was a good idea, though. He said it would be giving in, and what he's supposed to be learning is self-control. "I can't let my stomach or my feelings run my life," he said. I'm pretty sure he was saying it for my benefit.

Shane's become a model member of his new Foods group, by the way. Mr. Melnyk watches him like a hawk, but, still, you should have seen Shane on shortbread day. He wore an apron, and creamed eggs and sugar like he was the star of his own cooking show.

I still don't trust him, though. He's blamed everything on Bonnie – almost like she had him under her spell, and he couldn't help himself. That's even what he said in his letter to me. "Dear Nell," he wrote. "I'm sorry for what I did. I guess I was acting under Bonnie's influence. But I'm going to change now. I'll never do anything like that to you again." He signed it, "Sincerely, Shane Morrison," and didn't add any graphics.

Shane says Bonnie put the dead mouse through Uncle Martin's front door. He was at a hockey game with his dad and had nothing to do with it. He does admit that he got a friend of his to hang the catnip mouse in my locker. "But it was Bonnie's idea," he said. Then he made a big deal of refusing to name the kid who actually did the job. "I'm sorry," he said, like he was Robin Hood or somebody lofty like that. "I can't inform on a friend."

I think I've come pretty far with trusting people. And I'm sure Shane won't do the SAME thing again, to me, or probably to anybody else. But I do believe he'll do something else, if he can get away with it. Some people never seem to get the message.

*I*use the front door at school these days, like most everybody else. Mr. Wills is standing there today, like he usually is, and he nods at me as I leave. It's Hat Day, and he's wearing an Edmonton Trappers ball cap. He has it on backwards, to show he's with it, and his ears look very perky.

I wore a toque, but I took it off after first period because it made me hot. I looked in my locker mirror, and my hair was standing on end like I'd put my finger in an electric socket, but I decided it looked interesting. Anyway, I knew gravity would take over, eventually, and settle it down.

The air feels nippy when I step outside the school, so I put my toque on again. There's no snow on the ground yet, but I can see my breath and I know it's coming. In one of her e-mails, my mom said that Edin only had a thin jacket to wear, and sandals with no socks. She said when it got cold, it would be tough for him. I guess that's not true any more.

As I'm waiting for the lights to change at 111th Avenue, I realize that I don't think about red flags and explosions as much as I used to. What I think a lot about now, is Mom coming home for two weeks over Christmas. Uncle Martin kept his promise and didn't call her about the bad part of Remembrance Day. I e-mailed her myself, when I was feeling clear about what happened.

It's going to be a difficult Christmas for Mikey. Mom's waiting to tell him about Edin until she gets home. Of course, all the books and stuff the kids at Mary Chase sent will help other kids – but not the one he's been thinking about. I know he'll need to have lots of her attention.

But I'll need time with her too. There's stuff I want to talk to her about, like changing schools, and how hard it is to say goodbye, and like how you're supposed to handle it when someone does something to you that really hurts a lot. I wonder how Edin's brother feels about the people who buried all those land mines. I also wonder – although it comes out of nowhere – if Mom's forgiven Dad for walking out on us. I haven't wanted to talk much about it since I've been old enough to understand. Now, though, I'd like to. If she's been able to get rid of her bad feelings, maybe she can tell me how she went about it. Then – when I'm ready, of course – maybe I'll be able to think the way she does about my father. And the way Sam wants me to about Bonnie.

I'm pretty sure my mom will be able to help me. She's lived through some rough times. And after all, she IS a peacekeeper.

Subject:	**To Nell Hopkins – PRIVATE**
Date:	December 1, 2000 20:10:37
From:	"MCpl.AS.Mackelwain,ASU Edmonton,
	582-5418,0900" <mail466@dnd.ca>
To:	mmackelwain@hotmail.com

Dear Nell,

I made this private, because I didn't want Martin to read it. I'm glad you're concerned about his relationship with Christine. She sounds like a wonderful person, though, and I don't think she'll be really hard on him. I know he's a little eccentric, and I'm sure you can't imagine this, but she might actually like him. Stranger things have happened.

I also made this letter private, because I should have made time to write to you and Lester B. separately all along, instead of together. I'm looking forward to spending time with you too. There are so many people here from Edmonton that we've put up a Whyte Ave. street sign in front of the mess. Every time I look at it, I think how much I'd like to go there with you when I get home. The Christmas lights will be up and we can have hot chocolate and pastries in that café with the comfortable chairs. Will you go with me?

I haven't been to the V.K. school recently, but Lorna says that about six of the older girls there are working on a thank-you present for us because of the work we've done. It's a lip-sync to a song by Britney Spears. They don't understand much of what they're saying, but Lorna tells me they have the pronunciation down pat.

I'm looking forward to coming home.

Love You,

Mom

"MCpl.AS.Mackelwain,ASU Edmonton,582-5418,0900"

e-mail:466@dnd.ca

Acknowledgments

*M*y sincere thanks and admiration go to Master Corporal Leanne Karoles, a Canadian peacekeeper in Bosnia from September, 2000, to April, 2001. Her willingness to share memories of that time has been essential in the writing of this book.

I'm also grateful to Rafaella Montemurro, Anne McGrath, Naja Asif, and Sergeant Jeff Wilkes of Edmonton Police Services, all of whom contributed in some way to the shaping of this book; to Glen Huser, Mary Woodbury, Linda Collier, and Joseph Wood for personal and professional support; to Coteau Books for seeing value in the early drafts of the story; and to Barbara Sapergia, an editor from heaven.

About the Author

*D*ianne Linden is a writer and editor who has worked for many years as a teacher and educational consultant. Her work has been published in many literary magazines, and anthologized in Canada and Britain. She has co-created and/or edited *Running Barefoot: Women Write the Land* and the poetry-comic *Faux Paws,* as well as literature for teachers. *Peacekeepers* is her first book of fiction.

Dianne grew up in Colorado and lived in the Eastern United States and Germany before moving to Edmonton, which she now considers home.